Seasons of the Broken Arrow

G S Guy

Penheart Publishing

Published by Penheart Publishing
107 McCarthy-Cook Circle
Middleburgh, NY 12122

www.penheartpublishing.com

Seasons of the Broken Arrow is a work of fiction. However, some names and locations are based on the lives of real historical figures.

Published and printed in the United States of America.

ISBN – 13: 978-0615978888
ISBN – 10: 0615978886

To my wife Christine

Without her words of encouragement, hard work, and continued support, this book would not have been possible.

For my amazing son, Devyn

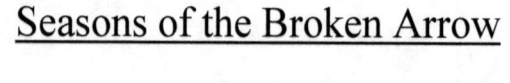

Seasons of the Broken Arrow

Part I

<u>October 25, 1781—The Battle at Fort Johnstown,</u>

<u>New York</u>

Chapter I

The woodsman staggered through the morning mist that blanketed the entire forest. Holding his side he struggled to keep moving, but every laborious step nagged at the arrow that protruded from his buckskin coat.

"Damn it!" he moaned. He fell to his knees and collapsed alongside the trunk of a decaying oak. Angling himself into a half-sitting position, he gently opened the torn leather where the arrow had pierced his jacket. Beyond the fog of his breath he saw his undershirt soaked with blood.

The man groaned as he grasped the wooden shaft and tried to pull it out. The barbs of the arrowhead were deeply lodged between his ribs and wouldn't budge. He was getting weaker by the second and his vision started to blur. The excruciating pain in his side grew more intense with every breath.

Half conscious and shivering from the cold, everything around him seemed to become eerily peaceful, except for the sounds of musket-fire and the shouts of frenzied men in the near distance. The battle was closing in on him, and he knew that if he didn't keep moving *they* would pick up his trail and find him within minutes. Yet, he couldn't go any further. As it was, he was struggling to stay awake.

And that's when he saw them.

Ghostlike shadows rapidly weaving in and out through the tall trees. He fumbled for his knife and readied himself as best he could.

Meanwhile, the two warriors had been relentlessly tracking him. And even though they were able to gather his flintlock, pistol, and other personal items from the battlefield, locating him was still difficult.

Slowly urging their horses forward—and being careful not to utter a sound—their eyes scanned the ground with intense concentration, searching for clues of a freshly embedded footpath. Their presence in the woods would have been completely obscured if not for the sound of their horses' hooves stirring up the damp, autumn-colored leaves.

Manendra, the highest-ranking tribesman of the Turtle Clan, rode slightly ahead of his son. Out of respect, Alok always kept in tow of his father except during peaceful times when they were hunting for game. And because they were rarely ever seen apart, and due to their great likeness in appearance (many who first encountered the pair thought them to be brothers, despite their significant difference in age), the people of the clan lightheartedly referred to them as "one hawk with two heads."

Alok loved and admired his father deeply, yet at times suspected that the feelings weren't mutual. Although this couldn't have been further from the truth, he felt he needed to prove his worthiness to Manendra, which occasionally led Alok to become extremely insubordinate toward his father. And this day was no exception.

As they gradually rounded a rock wall and reached the top of a knoll, Manendra unexpectedly halted his horse and motioned for Alok to stop. His trained senses picked up a distinct sound unnatural to their surroundings. Squinting into the dense fog and turning his head sharply to where the slight noise had come from, his eyes fixated on a small clearing. Then, with vision as keen as an eagle scouting for prey, he saw what appeared to be some movement.

Manendra rapidly fisted his chest to gain Alok's attention and motioned with his hand. Without warning, and to Manendra's dismay, Alok jabbed his heels into the sides of his horse and quickly advanced ahead.

Upon reaching the site, Alok reared his horse and in one swift motion slid off its back, armed with a war hatchet. With the agility of a fleeting deer, he hurdled over the network of dead branches that littered the ground and was standing over his adversary in no time. Kicking the knife out of the wounded man's fist and grabbing the thick of his hair, Alok let out a great battle cry and raised his tomahawk to strike him a fatal blow.

With the last of his strength, the trembling man looked up into Alok's unrelenting eyes and gruffly yelled in fluent Mohawk, "*I am White Bear!*"

Stunned by the sudden outburst, Alok hesitated, but quickly

regained his wits. "Then you are a *traitor*...and now you will die!"

Manendra, now on foot and quickly advancing toward them, threw up his hand just as Alok was about to strike.

"Alok...Stop!" he commanded.

Still wielding the weapon above his head, Alok turned at the sound of his father's voice. "Why do you stop me?" he bellowed in his native language.

"He speaks the tongue of the Kanien-ke-ha-ka," reminded Manendra. "In doing so, he is entitled to stand trial before the three chiefs!"

Manendra placed himself between the two of them, held up his arm, and looked at his son with a foreboding stare that made Alok very uncomfortable.

"It is not our place to pass judgment upon men in the presence of the mountain God, *Kedar*." He looked into the northern sky, then back at his son. "We must not anger him—for fear of what may happen to our people!"

Alok lowered the weapon and adjusted his stance to fully face his father, while keeping a firm hold of the man's locks.

"I, *too*, hear that he speaks the language of the Mohawk," he retorted, jabbing his hatchet before him. "Yet I am not deaf...*or* blind! My father cannot see that his obedience lies with the bluecoats. He forgets that his enemies were once allies to the Kanien-ke-ha-ka! The same allies that raped our people, handed us lies, and stole the land that was once promised to our people by the Englishman John-son!"

Alok, now burning with rage at the sound of his own words, violently spit on the man, who was unaware of his dilemma and murmuring incoherently.

"Why is this murdering thief any better than the dogs that lie at the feet of the white one they call Wash-ing-ton?" he demanded.

Manendra did not answer. The situation was becoming more delicate with every passing second. He knew he had to divert Alok's attention away from their captive while finding a way to calm him. It was never an easy task.

Ever since he was a young boy, Alok became riled and even unstable if he didn't get his way. Even so, Manendra could usually diffuse his son's tantrums with soft-spoken words of reason. However, as Alok reached manhood, this was no longer the solution. Convincing Alok to choose the right path became a more daunting and tiresome task, especially during the heat of conflict. Yet, Manendra always seemed to find a clever way to discourage his only son's ill intentions before things escalated out of control.

Manendra stood tall when addressing Alok, raising his chin slightly to demonstrate authority. "Why is it that my son cannot see that he is not like the others?" he said calmly, but firmly.

Alok pursed his lips so that he wouldn't interrupt his father. Instead, he inflated his chest to show strength and breathed heavily through flared nostrils.

"Look!" Manendra pointed down at the man. "He covers himself with the skins of our brother, *Zev!*"

Manendra knelt down next to the man and grasped one of his pant leggings to reveal the faded, though obvious, tribal markings.

"He colors his dress as the people of the Turtle do," he continued as he stood up. "If he is who he claims to be, then it is for the council to decide whether he lives...or whether he dies!"

"Humph!" grunted Alok, unwillingly caving in to his father's reasoning. He knew when it was wise to back down, because Manendra had a breaking point. Something that Alok would never be responsible for again, since he had done so in the past and regretted it ever since. And today, he could have easily caused Manendra to pass that threshold, but he couldn't help himself. He hated those who were against *his* people and he wanted nothing more than to be rid of them all...one way or another.

Manendra, in contrast, was more compassionate toward his captives and believed that *all* men should be given the right to justice. Unlike his father, Alok couldn't tolerate any sympathy to the enemy, and had the reputation of being quick tempered if justice wasn't served cold enough for his liking.

On more than one occasion, Alok tried to convince the elders why their enemies should never be given refuge, but instead the end of a tomahawk. In his mind, negotiating with one's enemies meant weakness. A weakness, he forewarned, that would undoubtedly compromise the existence of the remaining tribes of the Five Nations. To Alok, it was about the hunter and the hunted. One must surely die so that the other could live.

In any event, Alok felt as though he should at least entertain his father. That is, until Manendra finished lecturing him. And when he felt it safe to interject, he heartily replied, "Then he is Manendra's to deal with!" Not to be completely outdone, he stepped toward the incoherent wretch and walloped him on the forehead with the hammer end of his hatchet.

"*Uughk*," groaned the man as his body went limp, instantly propelling him into a deep state of unconsciousness.

"He will surely die anyway," Alok fumed as he released the woodsman's hair with a forceful shove. "Manendra's heart is soft! Manendra, *my father*, is a fool!"

Alok furiously trudged the short distance back to his horse, mounted, and gave Manendra a glare of disapproval before maneuvering his way back toward the battle. His excited yelps echoed through the forest while Manendra turned his attention back to the injured man.

Manendra elevated the woodsman's bearded jaw and shifted his head from side to side to examine his features more thoroughly. A wave of puzzlement spread across his painted war-face.

I have seen this day many times in my dreams, he thought to himself, as he rolled the man's head back and forth. *Is it possible that these dreams were not just dreams, but visions of a time to come? If you are my lost son, then I will find truth in your words.*

Manendra carefully lowered the man's chin until it rested upon his chest. He took hold of the man's left wrist and extended his limp arm. He pushed the shirt and coat sleeves beyond the elbow to expose the forearm's bare skin.

It was true. The unmistakable scar that marked his flesh was undeniable. Manendra cocked his head in disbelief before slowly standing.

"*Nicholas?*" he said quietly.

Manendra stared down at him for a few short moments, contemplating the poor soul's grave condition. Then, without sparing any more time, he jogged back to his horse to grab a leather flask of water and hurried back to the man's aid. Manendra crouched next to him and tore open his coat and shirt to fully disclose the apparently mortal wound.

Manendra removed a small pouch clasped to a beaded necklace from around his neck. It was filled with medicinal root powder. He mixed the powder with some water to form a greenish-black paste. Gently packing the mixture in and around the flesh where the arrow had made its entrance, Manendra was able to control the bleeding, and while doing so, chanted a healing sermon to awaken the sympathetic Gods.

Satisfied with his labor when he saw the blood begin to dry and clot, Manendra scavenged the forest floor for earthly materials. He fabricated a crude stretcher from leather straps and tree branches strong enough to support the man's weight. He skillfully attached the stretcher to his horse and lay Nicholas on top, covering him with the horse blanket for warmth.

Manendra knelt on the soft ground, and with outstretched arms, looked to the sky and sang a short psalm of gratitude. When finished, he sprang on the back of his horse and headed southwest to avoid the ensuing battle. Before long, he disappeared into the denser and safer part of the forest, and traveled in the direction of the Great River that flowed through the lush plains of the Canajoharie Valley.

Part II

Nicholas

When a boy becomes a man.

Chapter II

Nicholas barely heard the ladder creak under his mother's footsteps. She always came up to check on him and make sure he didn't fall asleep with the lamp still burning while reading his books. Tonight he was wide awake, though. He had just finished reading *Robinson Crusoe*, and with hands tucked under his head, blankly stared at the dimly lit ceiling imagining he was stranded on a faraway tropical island. A far cry from his home tucked in the southern foothills of the Adirondack Mountains.

"Nice to see that you're still awake," his mother lightly chided, as she stooped over and sat next to him on his bed.

"Oh, hello Mother," Nicholas said with a smile. "I was just..."

"I know what you were *just* doing, Nicholas Dunne," she replied, motioning for him to sit up so she could fluff his pillow. "You were fantasizing instead of sleeping. What will become of you and that imagination of yours?"

She gently pushed on his shoulder to make him lie back.

"You know," she said, "if your father were here he would..."

"But he's not!" blurted Nicholas. "He promised me that he would be home two days ago! How much longer, Mother?"

"Any time now, I suppose," she said, trying not to show any signs of concern. "You know he had a lot of business to take care of in Albany, but I'm sure he's on his way home at this very moment."

Nicholas sighed.

"In the meantime, it's up to us to mind the chores and keep up with *our* studies," she said matter-of-factly, touching the end of his nose with her finger. "Your father is going to be very tired when he arrives and will surely need lots of rest. So...that being said," she smiled, and pulled out a small black book from her apron pocket, "I thought this may help you pass the time while you wait."

Nicholas's eyes widened with enthusiasm.

"Mother!" he exclaimed. "When did you..."

"Never mind that," she grinned, as he excitedly flipped through the pages. "It's *Defoe's* next volume. I asked Mr. Cosselman to order it from New York weeks ago, because he knows how impatient you are."

"But we don't have the money," Nicholas said, looking back at her, "and Father said only to use any money that we have..."

"Never mind your father," she interrupted. "Besides, it was a little money I had put aside for just such an occasion. And you know your father would rather see you pass the time away reading rather than spending it all day at the lake, right?"

Did he ever. Nicholas deeply adored his father and thought he was probably the strongest and most intelligent man he ever knew. A full-blooded Irishman, his stature was unusually large—*probably several inches beyond six feet*, Nicholas guessed—and yet anyone who was fortunate enough to make his acquaintance soon found out that his big heart and magnetic charm made him very likeable. So much so, that close friends usually called him "Tibbs", or "Tibby"—a sort of nickname meaning *Tender Irish Bull*. A name his mother never got used to whenever it was substituted for his Christian name, *Patrick*.

His father's virtues were hard work, good common sense, and being neighborly and charitable to others less fortunate than they. All characteristics and values he had acquired during his childhood.

***

As a lad of twelve or so, Patrick sailed across the Atlantic to America as a cabin boy on a merchant ship owned by his Uncle Francis (a childless and widowed relative from Philadelphia). Because his uncle was quite wealthy and respected throughout the community, Patrick's parents agreed that only *he* could supply their son with a proper education—one that his father could never dream to provide him on a mere sheepherder's wage. So, plans were arranged by correspondence and Patrick was soon waving goodbye to his parents from aboard the vessel *Dublin*, bound for the New America.

Pat—as his uncle from Philadelphia affectionately called him—was received with open arms and soon set on a course to a promising future. Nicholas's father always spoke highly of his Uncle Francis, and notably considered him his "mentor." Yet, in the same breath, he also jokingly referred to him as "...the jolly, fat type of fellow whose appetite was larger than his purse." He could always make his son laugh when he told stories of his uncle whom, sadly, Nicholas would never have the pleasure to know.

In later years, as a highly educated young man in his mid-twenties, Patrick became interested in politics and developing land patents. With help from his uncle's unending list of well-respected and powerful business associates—who happened to be directly linked to the King of England himself—Patrick was formally given the title of "Colonial Surveyor" under the direct scrutiny of the British Crown.

Shortly thereafter, he attended an informal political dinner engagement on the outskirts of Philadelphia, where he was introduced to a young and strikingly beautiful woman named Catherine.

Cate, as she was almost always called, happened to be a prominent socialite whose father owned the largest trading company in the city. It was no wonder that her parents became worried when Patrick called on her from time to time. They had hoped for a more "suitable gentleman" who could provide their only daughter with the things that they thought Patrick would never be able to afford her. Yet none of that interested Cate, especially after being captivated by Patrick's unending charm and good-natured wit.

So, in time, it became quite obvious that the pair had fallen deeply in love with one another and would soon thereafter become engaged. Within the following year, and to the consternation of Cate's parents, they were married.

Patrick and Catherine Dunne enjoyed every minute of their newlywed lives together. Though not long after their vows, Patrick was given an assignment to relocate to upstate New York. He was to meet up with one Major William Johnson for further instructions, which turned out to be the mapping and claiming of territorial boundaries for the British Empire above the small community of John's Town. Cate's parents were utterly disappointed by the news, to say the least. They pleaded with her to stay because they feared for her safety within the vast and unexplored northern wilderness. Yet, strong-headed as she was, she firmly stood her ground, saying, "My place is with my husband," and, "It would be unloving to leave his side when he needs me now more than ever."

They left Philadelphia, and after an arduous journey, eventually arrived at Fort Hunter on the Mohawk River (which happened to be a run-down military post hardly fit to accommodate soldiers, much less traveling civilians). They met up with a small regiment of armed soldiers and local Indians who would guide and protect them while traveling to the Major's settlement. Hastily, they set out the same day they arrived, for the mere thought of spending even one night at the parasite-infested post was too unsettling to contemplate.

Without incident, they arrived at a large manor pinned neatly between two blockhouses named Johnson Hall, which was situated on the northern outskirts of John's Town. There, they were cordially greeted by the Major himself.

That same night, after an impressive welcoming banquet, the appointed men discussed and charted plans to navigate the unexplored regions to the north. During this time, Major Johnson advised Patrick to establish some land for a new home within arm's reach of the town's fortifications. He explained that the French Army and their Canadian Indian counterparts were sometimes spotted in the area and could become hostile toward wandering pioneers.

With much persuasion, Patrick tried to convince the reluctant Major to grant him the right to settle deeper into the mountainous foothills of the Adirondacks, near the lakes of Garoga—an old and deserted Indian settlement—where his work could be completed in a more timely fashion. The Major finally endorsed the request, but only with the understanding that Patrick and his wife would have little protection from any threats. He also made it clear that the Crown could not, and would not, be held accountable for any "unforeseen" or "dire" circumstances regarding the progress of his work or, more importantly, their well-being. With both parties satisfied with the conditions, an accord was made with the swipe of a pen and a formal handshake.

Patrick and Cate set out for their destination within the week. They were readily supplied with a team of horses, a wagon full of provisions, and enough animals and fowl to sustain a comfortable, though solitary existence.

Their journey would take nearly four bug-ridden hours in the sticky July heat, traveling on a deeply rutted military trail. With twenty guards and ten Mohawk scouts to lead them, Patrick kept close to his wife until the twin lakes of Garoga reflected through the pines. Then, he rode ahead of the small party to locate an ideal location to stake a claim, which he had little trouble finding.

The obvious choice was a flat, open spit of land settled by Indians years ago, before they eventually migrated further south to take advantage of the vast and highly accessible waterways. The soil was rich and would be perfect for cultivating as soon as the rocks were cleared. There were plenty of beasts to hunt, and the lakes would provide an abundant supply of fish.

Though it wasn't much to look at, Patrick was thrilled with the prospect of it all. Cate, on the other hand, saw nothing but hard work. Yet it would be worth every drop of sweat if it meant the promise of an early and quite comfortable retirement, compliments of the Sovereign King. So they spared no time and went right to work.

The small army provided by the Major, and a few of their new Indian friends who stayed behind and pitched in alongside them, were able to complete what became a small village in itself. There was a mill situated next to a fast-flowing creek for grinding and sawing, which helped in the construction of a grand cabin made of logs and planed timber. To the east was a very sizable barn to house fowl and plenty of livestock. There was a horse stable, carriage house, and blacksmith shop to the west. A well and other small buildings for storage and curing meat were also constructed. The landscape seemed to have been created by the brush of a talented artist, and was eventually christened *"Dunne's Flats."*

Everything was completed by late September and the Major's men soon thereafter departed, leaving behind only a hired hand and a few Indian scouts for protection. What seemed like a difficult and hardened life would be just the opposite. Cate was quite comfortable with many possessions of her own, which were shipped from Philadelphia by her parents. She had many things in and around the home to keep her occupied, yet something was still missing in her life. And she knew what that was.

Cate longed for a child. A child to help avoid the loneliness she felt while Patrick was away on business.

Otherwise, all was peaceful for the time being and life would have become almost too monotonous if not for the company of the

Indians. Patrick and Cate soon became great friends with them, as they were a very kind people and quite knowledgeable about farming and hunting. They not only grew accustomed to the Indians companionship, but also adopted some of their ways.

Patrick grew fond of one Indian in particular. He was known as Manendra to his people and the colonists. Very few knew of his given Christian name, *Joseph*. Patrick chose him as his leading scout when navigating the forests and narrow waterways, since he spoke in broken, yet comprehensible, English. It wasn't long before they became very close friends and Patrick wouldn't survey the lands without him...and certainly would never venture into the wilderness alone until Joseph returned from infrequent trips to his native village. Together, they explored and mapped many unknown parts of northern New York. They were an inseparable team.

Time in the mountains seemed to slip away, yet Patrick never forgot what his wife so desperately yearned for. He too felt it was time to be graced with a child.

Two years had passed before Nicholas was born. Giving birth had nearly taken Cate's life, but she felt a gift from Heaven was well worth any sacrifice.

From the start, Nicholas was a strong boy in mind, spirit, and body. And as the months turned into years, he made his parents very proud with everything he did. He was very independent and quite outgoing, which is why he spent much of his time with the natives (probably because of the great attention they gave him).

Like his mother and father, Nicholas in time became familiar with the Indian's culture and learned to speak their language with great fluency. The natives enjoyed his company and accepted him openly as "one of their own." When the Indians would take jaunts to their village, some of them would almost always bring back a gift for Nicholas along with supplies for his parents. To show his gratitude, Patrick would entertain them with a great celebration of food and drink, while Nicholas and his mother would cook and clean and tend to their horses. Nicholas took especially good care of Joseph's horse. Sometimes he was allowed to ride it within the boundaries of the homestead. Nicholas grew to love Joseph like a second father, and ever since he could remember had called him "Uncle."

The handful of Indians living with the Dunne family kept a watchful eye for Algonquin Indians, who traveled south from the Canadian territory to exchange pelts for rum and other English goods. There were stories of harassment and brutality toward new settlers, although such occurrences were rare. For the most part, things remained quiet at Garoga's twin lakes. Too quiet, sometimes, for an energetic boy like Nicholas. Even though his lessons, chores, and the nearby eastern lake kept him busy most of the time, he longed for something more exciting to pass the time.

***

Nicholas, still beaming with excitement over his new book, sat up and looked at Cate with much love. "Thank you, Mother!" he said gratefully, throwing his arms around her.

Nicholas adored her. Yet there were times he felt sorry for her. She worked hard around the small farm and never complained a bit. He knew that she did it for his father. She loved him deeply and would do anything for him.

Cate was a dainty and gentle woman, except when trying to coax a stray cow back to the barn. Nicholas would chuckle at the sight of her long blonde hair dangling about her dirtied face as she pushed on the beast, yelling, "*Move it, mule!*" But she always made sure that every supper was served with her best china, and she always dressed accordingly.

She was a mild-tempered parent, even when Nicholas was unruly at times, and always found the time to spoil him with candy when she could afford it. He loved her like no other. While his father was away, they would talk for hours and sometimes fish together. Being an only child and with no other children close by, she was his friend and only confidant.

"I can't wait to start the first chapter!" he said with fervor.

"That, my young prince, will have to wait until tomorrow," she reminded him firmly, but lovingly. "You have studies and chores in the morning."

"Yes, ma'am," he replied, and plopped himself back into the comfort of his bed. Then his mother stood up, fixed his covers, and gently kissed his forehead before extinguishing the lamp.

"Now get to sleep," she ordered with a light smirk as she started down the ladder.

"Ma?" he called, propping himself on one elbow.

"Yes Nicholas?" she replied, pausing on the ladder so that only the upper half of her body could be seen.

"I could do extra chores tomorrow instead of schoolwork. Besides, it's only addition and history day, and I already know all of that."

"Nicholas Dunne, you little swindler!" she exclaimed. "Only thirteen years old..."

"Almost fourteen," Nicholas reminded her, rolling his eyes.

"Yes," she acknowledged. "almost...and you should know better than to try and pull a fast one on your poor old mother! Tsk, tsk."

She shook her head with a slight grin and started down again. "Goodnight, son...and not a sound!"

"Yes Mother, goodnight," he mumbled and lay back on his pillow.

Through the large, framed window next to his bed, Nicholas stared into the starry summer sky and thought of the stories in his books. His mother was right. He probably did have a big imagination...but that was okay with him.

Someday I'll have my own stories to tell, he proclaimed to himself.

Nicholas smiled as he turned on his side, and was soon fast asleep.

Chapter III

On his way home from a quick swim in the lake, Nicholas sliced the air with a makeshift sword fashioned from a pointed stick he found along the wagon-rutted road. He pretended to be a commodore in the King's Royal Navy, fending off ghastly pirates who tried to overrun his ship.

"Take that, heathen!" he cried valiantly, slashing the emptiness in front of him. "And that!"

It was a role that he played over and over again to help pass the time while his father was away. Hopefully, Patrick would be waiting for him at home by now. Nicholas couldn't bear the thought of doing one more chore in the dreadful summer heat. If his father were back from his trip, his mother wouldn't dare ask him to do any work. She knew how anxious Nicholas was to see him, especially since his arrival was long overdue.

It was always a great reunion when his father returned, and Nicholas always felt relieved and safe when that day finally came. He could easily picture it in his mind—the three of them joyfully embracing. That's when his father would look down at him and say in a disheartening voice, "I'm sorry, Nick. I truly didn't have the time to bring anything home to you."

Nicholas couldn't help but smile. He knew his father wasn't fooling anyone with that old prank, and his mother would tilt her head with an expression that undoubtedly would have said, "Stop teasing the poor boy."

Then, grinning like a fox, Patrick would say, "Here...maybe this will cheer you up." Right on cue, not able to contain himself any longer, he would reach into his pack and pull out a crumpled package wrapped in brown paper and tied with twine. Nicholas could never unwrap the present quickly enough, and when he finally got it open he was never disappointed. Of course, there was something for Mother too.

And the stories! His father would tell of great adventures

during his travels, as he and his mother listened intently, dining on a fine meal that she always prepared for the occasion.

It was going to be a great celebration! Nicholas forgot all about slaying pirates and started to run the last fifty yards home.

Just beyond the bend their cabin would come into full view, yet something in the corner of Nicholas's eye caught his attention…just enough for him to turn his head. He slowed and then stopped for a brief moment to peer into the dense woods on both sides of the road. A mild sense of uneasiness spread through him and the hair on the back of his neck stood up. It was almost as if something…or someone…was watching him!

He scanned the woods on each side, still not seeing anything out of the ordinary. He thought to himself, *Probably just a deer or somethin'*, and shrugged it off.

Nicholas slowly moved forward, but didn't get very far before once again stopping in his tracks. This time he distinctly heard yelps and whoops of what sounded like Indians echoing through the trees. Then the shrill cry of a woman's voice pierced the air.

"That was Mother!" Nicholas said worriedly, focusing all his attention in the direction of the sounds. Something was dreadfully wrong.

He bolted and ran as fast as he could. He swore that he saw a rider-less horse galloping through the woods and going in the opposite direction, which seemed very odd.

Reaching the bend, he came to a complete halt on the edge of the property. With great alarm, he saw Indians frantically scouring about the yard. These were not the Mohawk Indians that he was so accustomed to. They were different. Very different!

He saw his father running from the barn toward the cabin. His shirt was torn and bloodied, his trousers soiled with dirt. An Indian was chasing him. Nicholas flung himself into the thick brush that lined the forest's edge. He carefully lifted his head.

"Cate!" his father screamed. "Get to the house! NOW!"

Then, the warrior flung his hatchet, which found its mark in his father's back. With outstretched arms he fell lifelessly to the ground, not far from the corpse of another Indian face down in the dirt.

His heart pounding wildly, Nicholas felt he should do

something...anything! But it was no use. He was paralyzed by fear and could only watch.

There was another scream and he jerked his head around. His mother was running as fast as she could, holding up her dress with both hands. One of the warriors appeared out of nowhere and was on her with his tomahawk. He viciously hammered her skull, and Nicholas watched her fall to the ground and convulse violently. The Indian dropped to one knee and clutched her long blonde hair. With his knife, he cut her scalp and yanked the hair hard, releasing it from the blood-soaked bone underneath. Raising it toward the sky, he yelped victoriously.

It felt like a horrible dream. Nicholas wanted to wake up and wanted to get away, yet he was too terrified to leave the safety of the brush. All he could do now was hope he wouldn't be discovered.

He watched as the invaders ran roughshod through their worldly possessions and rounded up the frantic animals. Thick, acrid smoke filled the air and Nicholas immediately felt ill. Everything was on fire; the cabin, barn, and outer buildings. He keeled over and cupped his mouth before expelling the contents of his stomach. He started to cry and tried not to choke on his vomit.

When there was nothing left to heave up, Nicholas wiped his lips. He decided to make a dash for it. He slowly made his way back to the road. He looked back to make sure that it was safe, but one of the Indians spotted him and yelled something to his allies.

Instantly, they started after him. An arrow from the opposite direction sliced through the air, barely missing Nicholas's head. One of his pursuers was struck in the chest and dropped dead. Nicholas was stupefied, but it gave him the perfect opportunity to get away.

It seemed like he ran for an eternity, until he saw another Indian on horseback directly ahead of him. Nicholas shrieked and tried to escape through the trees, but the attempt was futile. He could hear the horse rapidly gaining on him. He glanced back. The rider was leaning forward with one arm outstretched. A hand grabbed the back of his shirt and easily elevated him from the ground.

"Let me go!" Nicholas screamed, as the rider threw him over the horse's bony spine. He tried to worm his way from the grip, but the Indian had him tightly secured.

"Let me go!" he screamed again. The Indian ignored him, turned his horse back onto the trail, and headed south away from the mayhem.

It seemed like they rode forever at a full, pounding gallop until finally the Indian slowed his horse to a trot and turned back into the woods. Nicholas could clearly see the familiar lake where he often swam. The Indian stopped at the shore and got down from his horse. Nicholas tried to escape, but the Indian kept a tight grip on his shoulders.

"Nich-o-las!" the Indian said in broken English. "Nich-o-las!" he repeated louder, trying to shake some sense back in him. "It is I...Manendra!"

Nicholas tried to bite and scratch him.

"Uncle Jo-seph!" the Indian said louder.

Nicholas relaxed a little. He was relieved to see that it was indeed his father's good friend. Then he burst into tears and sobbed uncontrollably.

Bending down and shaking Nicholas's shoulders with both hands, Manendra commanded, "Look at me!"

Nicholas tried, but couldn't stop crying.

"Look at me!" he commanded again.

Nicholas straightened and tried to look at him through watery eyes.

"What is done, is done," said Manendra, "but you must be brave and stay quiet!"

And for reasons Nicholas didn't understand, that's exactly what he did. The tears ceased and he became quite calm.

"We will leave now," Manendra said, hoisting Nicholas back up on the horse. He led the animal on foot along the shoreline to a small narrow path into the woods. Without saying a word, Manendra hopped onto the horse and charged through the forest. Nicholas had to duck branches that nearly whipped his head. He feared falling off at any moment.

After many hours of riding, Manendra finally stopped his horse and lowered Nicholas to the ground before dismounting.

"We are safe now," he said, looking through the trees. "We are close to my village and will walk, so the horse can rest." Manendra handed a leather water flask to Nicholas. "Drink, but be silent," he cautioned.

Nicholas took a few gulps. The water felt good in his dry, pasty mouth, still tasting of acid. Manendra also drank, then they hiked a downward slope.

They walked for about two miles before getting back on Manendra's horse. It was then that Nicholas could smell sweet, pungent smoke wafting through the air. He heard a dog bark and then what sounded like children playing nearby. Through the trees he saw ripples of water reflecting the setting sun.

As they neared the edge of the forest, Nicholas saw a large Indian village come into view situated on the bank of an enormous river. There were tunnel-shaped structures covered in bark and measuring at least a hundred feet long. There were fires burning and people wandering about busying themselves.

As they drew nearer to the encampment, he saw canoes forged from fallen trees and docked upright upon the narrow, sandy shore. His father had told him about native villages situated along great rivers, but had only observed them from a distance. This one was exactly how Nicholas had pictured it...and, at the same time, unlike anything he had ever seen before.

Chapter IV

Manendra and Nicholas were being observed as they rode into the center of the immense village. Some of the Indian children boldly came forward for a closer look, curious to know who their new guest was. Everyone's eyes were fixated on Nicholas, and he felt both uncomfortable and intrigued by the horde of spectators. Yet no one spoke to them, and Manendra kept his gaze forward, ignoring their audience.

Nicholas wasn't afraid, not with Manendra close to him, but he did wonder what was in store. It was hard to think and his head throbbed from the day's horrific events.

Manendra halted the skittish horse in front of one of the longhouses and slid from its sweaty back. He grabbed Nicholas by the waist and effortlessly lifted him to the ground with his powerful hands.

"Stay with the horse," he said, handing the reins to Nicholas. Then he disappeared into the longhouse's dark entryway.

Nicholas did as he said and stood next to the animal, while some of the children and adults gathered round him. One of the Indian boys confidently walked up to him and cautiously reached out to touch his shirt. Nicholas whipped his shoulder back and slapped the hand away. The startled boy looked at him with a crinkled brow.

Nicholas scanned the crowd. The younger ones had wormed their way to the front, while some of the shorter men in back stood on their toes and craned their necks to get a better view. Everyone waited in anticipation for what might happen next.

Again the Indian boy reached out, this time to touch Nicholas's blonde hair. The white boy angrily smacked the hand a second time and raised his clenched fists in defense. The Indian boy backed into the crowd, unsure what to think.

Manendra reappeared from the longhouse and motioned for Nicholas to follow him. But Nicholas hardly acknowledged him and didn't make a move, keeping his attention focused on everyone half-circled around him.

"Nich-o-las, come!" Manendra demanded in English, gesturing with his hand.

Nicholas slowly backed away from the crowd, keeping his fists clenched, and bumped into something behind him. Thinking that he was about to be assaulted from behind, he quickly swung around to find it was Manendra.

The Indian put a hand on his shoulder. "Do not be afraid, Nich-o-las. You are safe here...and no harm will come to you."

Nicholas lowered his fists, looked up at him, and calmly replied, "I am not afraid, Uncle Joseph...but they should be of me!" He looked back defiantly to make sure they had heard him.

"I have no doubt that they would be afraid...if they understood the language of the English tongue," Manendra chuckled with a slight hint of sarcasm. "After all, it would be unwise to tangle with a spirited white bear, would it not?" He cocked his head a little and more or less said to himself, "Hmm...White Bear. That is a *strong* name!"

Nicholas wasn't exactly sure what he meant, but he had an idea. All Indians were given names to reflect their true spirits, which Manendra taught him long ago, but he wasn't an Indian! *Maybe it was customary to give visitors an identity instead of referring to them by their Christian names. Maybe it was a sacred thing or something.* His brain was too heavy to think about it much more, and he followed Manendra to the doorway.

They crossed into the threshold of the building. It was almost pitch-black inside and Nicholas couldn't see from being in the bright sun. Even when his eyes adjusted, it was still difficult to make out what...or who...occupied the inside. The interior was barely lit by some daylight that streamed through narrow cracks of the twig and bark structure. He could make out two circular fire pits filled with coals, strategically centered near the front and back entryways. A hint of white smoke corkscrewed to the ceiling and escaped through small, square openings.

Sitting on colorful blankets were women and girls who were either weaving, cooking, or tending to infants. They pretended not to notice the visitors.

Manendra took Nicholas to one side of the house and pointed to a blanket folded on the ground.

"Sit here and wait," he instructed. "I will return soon."

Nicholas watched him disappear from the house, then looked at the women and girls to see if they were watching him. They weren't.

And then it hit him all at once.

Tears gushed from his eyes. His heart ached for his mother and father. He had lost all he had known. He was engulfed in rage. In between sobs his body tensed, lusting for revenge.

Nicholas barely noticed when the girl knelt next to him. She held out a carved wooden bowl that contained what looked like flat bread, cornmeal, and chunks of meat.

"Ikeks," said the girl.

Nicholas looked into her eyes, wiped his face, and became still. She was quite beautiful and looked about his age.

Her hair was as black as the night sky and her skin was tan and smooth. She wore a seamless leather skirt adorned with a colorful belt and a necklace made of small beads and dyed pieces of animal bone. Her boots were also made of leather and tied with rawhide laces.

"Ikeks," she repeated and made an eating gesture. Nicholas knew the word, as he understood a good part of her language. He took the bowl from her and nodded. She gave him a slight smile before shyly turning away.

He watched her walk back to the other side of the room. Her act of kindness gave him a glimmer of inner peace. And he *was* hungry. The wonderful aroma of the food made him realize that his stomach was growling. Roaring was more like it.

He eagerly shoveled the food into his mouth with his fingers. As the food filled his belly, it dawned on him that maybe, just maybe, he would get through it all somehow.

Nicholas had consumed every bit of food just before Manendra returned, and he was relieved to see him. He sprang to his feet and greeted him with a heartfelt hug (something he often did when Manendra returned home with his father from a long excursion). Yet this time, and to the boy's dismay, Manendra pushed him away. He saw the serious look in Manendra's eyes.

"We will go to the elders now," said the Indian in a sober tone. "You will not speak, but be silent."

Nicholas nodded. He was dumbfounded but not too worried.

Sure, Manendra's demeanor was strange to him, but his Uncle Joseph was the only person left in the world he could trust.

Exiting the longhouse and crossing the vast yard, they entered a smaller lodge. A roaring fire lit the interior, which was decorated with feathers, beads, and animal pelts. An assortment of weaponry and crafted artifacts hung in disarray on the walls.

Nicholas counted six braves sitting cross-legged around the fire. There was a vacant space just large enough for Manendra and him. Except for the crackling fire, it was quiet. Then one Indian spoke, peering somberly into the fire. Nicholas thought he was an elder due to his wrinkled, leathery face and the long pipe cradled in his arms.

"You are *White Bear*," he said to Nicholas, waving his hand near the flickering tongues of flame. "If it is agreed upon that you remain with our people, then you will become Manendra's adopted son."

Confounded, Nicholas looked at Manendra—who sat as straight as a statue—then back to the old man, whose deep voice became more audible and deliberate as he continued.

"If it is so, then you will learn the passageways of the High Spirit, and of the moon, and of the sun and land. You are a part of the Wolf, the Bear, and the Turtle; where the Wolf is cunning, the Bear is strong, and the Turtle wise. All parts make up the whole of the Mohawk peoples."

The chief looked up to the ceiling and then back into the immense fire.

"White Bear of the Turtle," he continued, "if it is decided, then Manendra, your new father, will show you the paths of our fathers, and of their fathers before them. This is the way of the Great One, and so, this too, will be known."

Nicholas watched him toss some kind of powder into the fire, which created a slew of rising sparks. The meeting was apparently over, as Manendra rose to his feet and waited for Nicholas to follow. They quietly left the dwelling without saying a word.

Outside it was nearly dark. When they returned to the longhouse, Manendra led him to a pile of blankets where he would apparently sleep.

Back home he was used to thick, soft quilts and a feathery

pillow. Here, the ground was hard and there was no pillow for his head, and the blankets were heavy and stiff. They had an unpleasant odor as well; a combination of decaying leaves and animal hair. But they were warm, and the minute he lay his head down he fell into a deep slumber.

Throughout the dreadful night, he became the main character in horrid nightmares. In one, he found himself lying in a pit of muddy slop while wild boars with large spiked teeth chomped at his legs. In another segment, frantic crows pecked at his eyes and wild-eyed Indians thrashed at him with claws as sharp as talons. And someone far away called to him in a familiar voice. That's when he woke, drenched in a cold sweat, screaming for his mother.

Disoriented, he looked around the darkness thinking that he should see the side table at his bed, the oil lamp he read by every night, the bureau in the corner, the walls fashioned of massive, rich-colored logs. Yet he couldn't see any of it, and when his senses returned to him his heart sank with the realization of his true whereabouts.

As haggard as he was from his descent into hellish dreams, the dawn was a thankful relief. Nicholas rubbed his eyes and wiped away the crust caked around his eyelids. He was somewhat mystified to see a boy, seemingly close to his age like the girl the day before, hunkered down next to him and watching him with an eerie stare. Nicholas, unsettled, sat up and slid back on his haunches.

"What is your name?" the boy said.

Nicholas cracked open his lips a bit, but didn't reply.

"I am Alok. What is your name?" the Indian boy repeated, growing a little more impatient.

He cleared his throat and said, "Nicholas...I am Nicholas."

It was evident that the boy didn't seem to really care about his name. Rather, he stood up and adjusted the loose belt around his waist. "It is time for us to eat now."

He left Nicholas by himself and walked over to the nearest fire, where other dwellers were huddled together. Nicholas looked for Manendra in vain. He rolled out of his blanket and went over to join the boy. He sat next to Alok just before a heavyset woman—who was distributing some sort of dense porridge from a small black kettle—

28

shuffled over and set a full bowl of the stuff in front of him. It was more cornmeal, which had the look and texture of paste. It hardly seemed edible yet, it smelled good, and Nicholas *was* pretty hungry.

He watched as the others dipped hands into their bowls and filled their mouths. Imitating them, Nicholas dug right in and found himself relishing his breakfast with one quick scoop after another. It was only after did he realize that they had stopped eating and were intently watching him. His mannerisms had apparently embarrassed them. He gingerly placed the empty bowl in front of him and waited patiently for Alok to finish.

Soon after, Alok got up, walked over to a large wicker basket, and placed his bowl inside. Nicholas did the same.

Alok sprinted outside and left Nicholas standing there, not knowing what to do next. One of the women pointed to the entrance, and with a bit of annoyance in her voice told him to leave. Realizing that he had just been reprimanded, Nicholas left the longhouse without hesitation.

It was a brisk, sunny day outside and a cool breeze caressed his face. All about the village the men were cutting wood, carving a canoe from a felled tree, and skinning pelts while engaged in conversation. He saw Manendra on horseback, his bow over his shoulder, leading some men into the forest. He supposed they were going hunting, since their horses were moving at a nonchalant pace.

At the far end of the village he could see a group of boys standing at the bank of the broad river, tossing lines into the slow moving water. His curiosity was piqued and he decided to join them.

One of the older boys asked if he would like to fish. Nicholas nodded and went down the steep, muddy bank only to find himself flat on his back as his feet flew out from under him. The boys laughed and Nicholas felt his face turn red. He picked himself up and wiped the mud from his trousers. The boys quickly lost interest in him and went back to fishing, all except for Alok, who gave him a sneering glance.

One of the taller boys pulled in his line and positioned himself at Nicholas's side.

"Here," he said, tying bait to the end of the string and offering it to Nicholas. "Can you fish?" he asked earnestly.

"I can fish," Nicholas said.

He watched as the others lobbed their lines into the water, and as he was feeling confident, gave it a go. He made a good first attempt, but instead of the bait sinking on contact, it bobbed with the downstream current and tangled with the other boys' lines. They all moaned and complained and Alok let out a short, disgust-filled sigh. After untangling the mess Nicholas had caused, Alok trudged over to him and took hold of his tackle. Pulling out a dark polished stone from his fishing pack, he looped the cord around a groove cut into the stone and secured it with a knot. Then he slapped the pole back into Nicholas's hand. Alok shook his head in disbelief and went back to claim his spot.

Nicholas noticed one of the boys whispering something in Alok's ear, while Alok nodded in agreement. The others chuckled and called Nicholas names under their breath, but nothing too harmful. They didn't realize he could understand almost every word they were saying. Still, it wasn't anything to get riled over and he let them have their fun. His pride had been damaged enough, and he didn't much care to make more enemies.

Throughout the morning, hardly any of the boys were having much luck. Nicholas didn't suppose he would fare any better. River fishing was a lot more difficult than fishing in a lake, and he was about to give up when there was a tug on his line. Nicholas immediately reeled in the slack. He saw the frenzied catch zigzagging under the clear water.

He pulled the flopping fish onto the shoreline. It was huge! Nicholas stepped on its tail and hooked two fingers into its gill. Holding up his prize, he saw that it was at least twenty inches or more! They rarely ever grew so big in the lake he used to fish.

All of the boys, with the exception of Alok, crowded around him to admire the fantastic catch. Nicholas held it high for all to see and touch. He wanted everyone to share in the excitement. Alok could have cared less, though, and Nicholas didn't understand why.

"Alok...look!" Nicholas yelled over to him. But the boy ignored him and kept fishing. No matter. Nicholas was too busy being the center of attention to give him much more thought. He unhooked the gasping fish, threw it over the bank, and tossed his freshly baited line back into the water. In no time he had another bite, and to

Nicholas's surprise, it was larger than the first.

"I got another one!" he shouted with excitement, yanking it onto the bank. Nicholas grabbed the fish with both hands as it wriggled between his knees.

He heard one of the boys laugh and say, "Alok's *brother* will eat better than him tonight."

The rest of them snickered, and that was all Alok could take. He threw down his pole, ran up the bank without looking back, and with great disgust shouted, "He is *not* my brother!"

Nicholas didn't know what to do as he watched Alok head back to the compound. He quickly gathered up his fish and ran after him. Before Alok covered half the distance back, Nicholas caught up with him, grabbed hold of his arm, and spun him around.

"Alok, wait!" he urged.

"Go away!" yelled Alok. He jerked his arm free from Nicholas's grip and stomped ahead.

Nicholas watched him reach the center of the village. Alok plopped himself down between two men who were stoking coals in a fire pit. The men said some things to him and Alok said something back while making obnoxious hand gestures at Nicholas. The men looked up and only stared at him.

Rage welled inside Nicholas. He threw his fish to the ground and yelled to no one in particular, "I didn't ask for any of this!" Then he took off running. He wasn't sure where he was escaping to, but he didn't care.

Nicholas reached the sanctuary of the woods and started to cry the minute his hand touched the first tree. It was all too much for him to handle. He thought that by running deeper into the forest, things would change. And they did...for a little while.

Chapter V

Nicholas perched himself atop a large boulder overlooking the river, his forehead resting on his arms. He had stopped crying a long time ago, but he couldn't get his mother and father out of his mind.

"Why did this have to happen to me? Why, God?" he asked aloud, knowing that there wouldn't be an answer. That would be a miracle...and miracles just didn't happen like that. He had already been sitting there for hours and had no clue where he would sleep, what he would eat, or where he would go. He certainly couldn't go back now.

"*White Bear?*" a voice called from within the forest.

Maybe he could follow the river to Albany, where his father so frequently traveled. Maybe someone there would recognize his name and help him out. Or maybe he could hop aboard a seagoing vessel, sort of like his father did as a child, and sail across the ocean to Ireland where he might find his grandparents or some other relative willing to take him in!

"*Nich-o-las!*" the voice boomed.

That's exactly what I'll do, he thought, lifting his head and feeling a little excited by a plan that was starting to form. *They would help me! Especially, after I tell them about all the dreadful things that happened!*

Nicholas scanned the bushes at the water's edge.

"First, though, I'll have to find some food," he said quietly, looking downriver as far as he could. "I suppose it will take me at least a few hours to walk to Albany from here, and I'm not gonna make it by going hungry."

His thoughts were abruptly disrupted when he heard the deep huff of a horse exhaling. Manendra maneuvered around the trees and rode toward him. Nicholas put his head down, not knowing if Manendra was going to lecture him and drag him back to the village.

Manendra left his horse in the woods, walked over, and sat next to Nicholas. He fixed his gaze beyond the far reaches of the river. He didn't say anything at first, and they both sat in silence for a long

32

while.

"I have seen the fish that you scooped from the river," Manendra finally said. "It will be a very good meal for the one who is lucky enough to eat it."

Nicholas didn't respond. After a short pause, Manendra tried again.

"Nich-o-las," he said without looking at him, "whatever you choose to do in life is your decision...and you should not be persuaded to do otherwise by anyone. But know this...to each of us there is a destiny. And however you reach that destiny I will be there for you, because you will always be my son...in this life, and in the next."

Manendra took a breath, as if his next words would be difficult.

"When you came into this world with life, there was a promise that bound our spirits together. A promise I made to your father...to watch over you if there was no one else to do so."

Manendra put a hand on Nicholas's knee.

"And I agreed, because it was also what I wished. And nothing has changed since that day. My words to you, as they were to your father, are true."

Nicholas didn't doubt him for a second. Manendra could never lie, even if he wanted to.

"It is not necessary for you to be the blood of my blood," he continued. "It is what lies in our hearts that joins us together. This is the way of my people...and now, the way of your people."

Nicholas looked up and waited for him to finish.

"These are my words," he continued, "for you to remember. Now, it is for you to decide, and find your own way."

Manendra put his arm around Nicholas.

"What is troubling White Bear so much that he cannot speak to Manendra?"

Nicholas scraped at the rock with a twig.

"What happened, Uncle Joseph?" he said solemnly. "Why did this have to happen?"

Manendra hugged him a little tighter.

"I can tell you these things," he said, "but these things you already know."

Nicholas wasn't sure what he meant, but wanted him to

continue, since talking to Manendra made him feel better.

"Some men fear what they don't understand. And these men will rid themselves of what makes them afraid. They do not understand that all men are the same. They do not see that only what they think makes them different. The Great Spirit weeps many tears for all men who hate. It makes men weak and turns their spirits hard. It spoils their hearts so that they cannot live in life, or in death, with peace and harmony."

Manendra raised an arm and looked to the sky.

"Men that do not hate are given peaceful things," he said as he drew an invisible cross in the air with his hand, "in this life and for all eternity."

"Joseph, what do you know about yesterday?" Nicholas asked. "I mean, how did you end up on the trail leading to our home?"

Manendra let out a faint sigh. It was evident that he was trying to cope with his own private mourning.

"I will tell you what I know...if you wish."

Feeling sympathetic, Nicholas almost told him not to, but then let him continue. Manendra lowered his head as he spoke.

"I met up with your father, at the dwelling of Major John-son, just as he was returning from a long journey. He was full of life and spoke with great happiness, because soon he would be reunited with you and your mother. I was to ride with him, but could not. The Major needed to make other arrangements with me. Your father did not choose to wait for me, because he grew too impatient. I knew this and said I would meet up with him at Garoga after my talks with the Major were finished. I did not know that there would be any sorrow along the way."

Manendra lifted his head.

"It wasn't until I saw you from in between the trees that I sensed something was wrong. That is when I heard the sounds that came from the end of the path, and I stopped to listen. I watched you from a distance...I started to fear for your safety. Then I watched my brothers to the north, as you must have done the same, take the life from all of them. I saw that they were of the Algonquin League, but these men were not my brothers as I had first thought."

Manendra rubbed his stiff neck and crossed his legs to get more comfortable.

"Many suns ago, the Mohawk were told of the *ones* who shamed their own people for their wickedness toward the innocent. Only the Spirit of Death followed them, and for this they were tossed out of their own tribe, and banned from their own nation. They are lost men who wander and take what they want, not what they need...to live."

Manendra looked up into the heavens and confessed, "My spirit is full of shame because I have taken the life of one who was once a brother to me. Yet, my heart is glad that you still live," he said, looking at Nicholas. "Happiness fills my spirit to know that I have kept your father's word...to watch over you as I promised with my words, since he too, was also my brother."

Nicholas stared into nothing. It seemed like Manendra's voice was far away as he pictured the events. And the words about his father made him feel better in a strange sort of way.

"Yesterday was filled with great sorrow. But tonight, there is new life," Manendra continued. "I went back to the place of your parents and we made three holes in the earth. We placed your father, and mother, and the man who worked for your father, back into the land from where they came. Their bodies rest under a tree of Life, which now bears the symbol of a cross and a turtle." Manendra reached out to the sky with an open hand. "There, they wait for the Son."

Nicholas looked up to the heavens as Manendra continued.

"Our own braves that have fallen were returned to the lands of the Mohawk, so they too can wait to sit with their fathers. But the one that fell from my arrow will not sit with his fathers. His body was halved and scattered in the mountains, so that the animals of the forest would eat him and keep him separated. Forever his spirit will wander, searching for all the parts of his body. But he will not find them. He will hear his fathers cry out to him in the darkness, and he will cry out for them, yet he will not be heard. It is his punishment in death."

Manendra reached into his knapsack and held out a brown, crumpled package bound with twine in front of Nicholas.

"This was your father's...and now it is yours," he said. "It was with him when he died."

35

Nicholas took the package and stared at it for a long moment. He unwrapped it and found two things; a black book and a knife. The book was another novel by *Defoe* and he instantly thought of his mother. Inside, there was an inscription in his father's handwriting:

To our dearest, beloved Son,

With the grace of God's hand, we hope you fulfill all of your hopes, wishes, and dreams—and that every day is more adventurous than the next!

With love,

Mother and Father

Nicholas closed his eyes hard. He remembered all the times they shared together—all the laughter and joy. Nothing could have prepared him for the pain he felt right now.

He set the book in his lap and slowly removed the knife from its dyed leather sheath. It was the finest knife he had ever seen. The blade was at least eight inches long and sharp enough to split a single hair. The handle was made of antler bone and crimped with silver rings on each end. Etched on each side was a harp—the symbol of his father's heritage.

While examining the book and knife, Nicholas couldn't help but think that these dear possessions were the only things he had left. They defined his whole existence.

Manendra allowed him a moment of silence before he stood, placed his hand affectionately on Nicholas's head, and said, "What will they say to you when you look to the sky?"

Nicholas knew that he meant his parents. He knew they would want him to do what was right, and somehow he already knew what that was. But it wasn't what he wanted.

"This is something only *you* will ever know. I have prayed that you will find your way, my son. I pray that you, who will forever be known as Nicholas to the English, and as White Bear to the Mohawk, will be wise and strong with a large heart toward all people. For this, I would be proud, as your father and mother are proud!"

Manendra turned and walked back to his horse. Nicholas looked at the darkening sky and then back to his book and knife. He sprang to his feet just as Manendra leapt onto his horse and had the chance to filter away.

"Uncle Joseph!" he cried out, barely audible.

Manendra had nearly disappeared into the woods before Nicholas took a deep breath and called out again, but this time with more force. "Father! Please don't leave me here!"

Nicholas cried uncontrollably as he ran toward Manendra. The Indian dismounted from his horse and held out open arms. Manendra savored the embrace as Nicholas clung to him. And it would be many years before Nicholas would ever shed another tear.

Chapter VI

It was a quiet ride back to the village. Nicholas was happy to have his arms around Manendra's waist. He was glad that he wouldn't have to strike out on his own. Not that he couldn't have taken care of himself, but this way seemed easier...and safer. He would have to learn a new way of life, which made him think about the inscription his father penned in his book. He *would* make the most of every day...if not for himself, then for his parents.

When they reached the camp it was already dark and very late. There was a lot of activity within the confines of the village, more so than the night before. Everyone was gathered outside where many fires were burning. There was a large bonfire glowing bright in the center of the village, and more Indians than he had ever seen. Hundreds more!

"Why are there so many people tonight, Uncle Joseph?" Nicholas asked, as they circled the perimeter and headed for the corral.

Calling Manendra by his Christian name was still far easier than calling him "Father." One day, perhaps, it wouldn't feel too awkward. After all, he had known Manendra a very long time...all his life, for that matter.

"It is the gathering of the three tribes," Manendra said. "Today, the people of the Wolf and the Bear have traveled to join their brother the Turtle, and tonight the three brothers will become one. Tomorrow, all the Mohawk people will journey to Major John-son's dwelling to discuss land treaties. For three days the Five Nations of the Iroquois will make camp in the yard of the Major, and for three days, all the people who have come to listen will be with great celebration."

Nicholas grew very excited. It had been a long time since he had seen Major Johnson. He could remember some of the very few visits to see the fortifications with his mother and father when he was between the ages of eight and thirteen. They were some of the only times he was ever permitted to leave home and be part of the sights and sounds of the town. It was always an exhilarating experience!

***

He remembered how grand the main house was the moment he took his first steps up the large stairs leading to the front double entrance. Inside, the house was decorated with fine furniture, carpets, and the most exquisite draperies. Beautiful paintings hung from the massive white walls, and there was a large stone fireplace in every room.

He thought about his first introduction to Major Johnson. He seemed larger than life at the time, and Nicholas liked him right from the start. His face was round, lightly powdered with talc, and he wore a pony-tailed wig. He was a cheery old fellow who shook Nicholas's small hand with a very strong grip. He reminded Nicholas of his great uncle from Philadelphia, or at least the way he envisioned him from his father's fond memories.

He also remembered the bright red coat that fully cloaked his upper torso, the pure white trousers, and black polished shoes strapped with shiny silver buckles. If it weren't for some slight pudginess in his midsection, he was the fitting portrait of a handsome British soldier.

But Nicholas didn't have much time to spend with the Major. After a brief visit, he was scooted off to the stables to look at the Major's prized steeds, which had been shipped directly from the King's palace in England. He always thought it was a ploy to get him out of the house so his parents could talk to the Major in peace. After all, they knew if Nicholas became bored and fidgety, he might have become a nuisance. Nicholas supposed that he would rather have been outside than listen to grownups talk about nothing that interested him anyway.

The more Nicholas thought about it, the more it dawned on him that there *was* someone else...someone he missed a great deal.

Abraham.

Abe (as he sometimes called him) had a matted, whitish-gray beard with hair to match. He seemed very old to Nicholas...and was probably the most peculiar person he had ever laid eyes on, since he was the first Negro Nicholas had ever seen.

Nicholas wouldn't forget that day. After being booted from the manor, he flew down the steps of the great house and ran over to the open threshold of the barn. He squinted into the shadowy interior and at first didn't see anyone. Then a voice came from the back, startling him.

"You gonna stand there all day lookin', or is you gonna help me tend to brushin' down this pony?"

Nicholas hid behind the door and gingerly peeked around. The stable boss dipped a large bristled implement into a bucket of water.

"Well, you comin'?" he asked, still bending over the pail and looking up at Nicholas with the whites of his eyes. "Ain't nothin' ta be scared 'bout...lessa course, you's afraid of hosses."

Nicholas wasn't afraid of any horse, and he took that as an invitation—or a dare—to join the old man, who now had his back to him and was wet-brushing the brownish-red hair of the tall, majestic beast.

"They's anotha brush over by that stall," he said with a thick drawl, nodding his head to where it was resting.

Nicholas grabbed the brush and dipped it in the water, as he had done so many times before when he took care of their horses at home.

With an old footstool he found nearby, he stood on the other side of the horse and brushed its coat, all the while trying to catch discreet glimpses of the stable boss. But the old man knew what he was up to, and whenever Nicholas tried to steal a peek at him, he'd stop brushing and stare back at him with eyes that looked as though they would pop right out of his head. Nicholas ducked below the horse, and just as he lifted his head for another look, the old man would shoot back another glance, wilder and more cockeyed than the last.

This game went on for a few more minutes until the man couldn't hold it in any longer and bust out laughing.

"Now then," he said, dropping his brush in the water and moving the bucket, "s'pose that'll be it for today. Let's see 'bout gettin' the ol' girl in her stall, so's Abraham can rest a spell...hmm?"

Nicholas stepped down, placed his brush in the bucket, and dried his hands on his shirt while the stooped man led the mare to its quarters.

"There...jus' fine," he said latching the gate. "Now we can si' down and get to knows one anotha."

Abraham picked up the footstool and placed it next to a large barrel covered with a thick horse blanket. He groaned as he stepped up on the stool and plopped down on the barrel.

"Sit right there, boy, so's we can talk some," he said, pointing with a crooked finger to a dusty chair, while he wiggled a bit to get more comfortable. Nicholas sat down to face him and found it hard not to stare at his appearance.

Abraham took a pipe from his leather vest and lit it. Nicholas watched as he puffed it a few times to get it going. Eventually he did, and the smell of sweet tobacco filled the air. Nicholas thought the aroma was quite pleasing as some of the smoke swirled his way.

"Name's Abraham Benjamin Jackson, from the south...born and raised," he said with pride. "Who might you be?"

Nicholas squirmed a little in his seat and placed his hands under his legs.

"Nicholas Dunne, sir...from Garoga. Born and raised," he mimicked.

"I sees, mm hmm. Yo' daddy Mr. Patrick?"

"Yes sir. Patrick Dunne."

"Well then," said Abraham, lifting his pipe from his lips and extending a thin hand, "pleased to make yo' acquaintance, Mr. Nicholas. Yo' daddy is a fine good man, yessa, and always kind to ol' Abraham."

Nicholas, trying to act like a grownup, shook the man's hand a little harder than he intended. Abraham smiled and gave him a quick wink.

And that's how their friendship began. They sat and talked, passing the time away. It was then that Nicholas learned how Abraham was once a slave on a large plantation in the "deep south", and sold to a businessman who resided in the great city of New York. It was there that Abe met the Major. Abraham wasn't too sure how Major Johnson was able to get him back to John's Town, but that's what he did, and Abe was pleased as ever to get away from the city life that had terrified him from the very start.

At first, Abraham was one of the servants of the house. That is, until the Major realized that Abraham wasn't very happy with his new position, even though Abe always said that things were "jus' fine."

Yet, the Major knew differently and tried to give him duties to make him feel happier. That's how the Major was. His home had to be as cheerful and comfortable as possible, since he entertained quite a bit. Even the Major's son was intentionally spoiled to keep him happy although, most of the time, this had adverse effects.

Meanwhile, Major Johnson soon discovered that Abraham had a knack for training and caring for horses.

One day he called on Abraham to discuss the matter privately in his den. He told Abraham that he was forever a free man, and with his new independence he could live wherever he chose. But not wanting to lose a good hand, Major Johnson presented Abe with the opportunity to stay on at the house. He was offered comfortable quarters in back of the stables and a handsome salary to go along with it. Not having any other place to go, Abraham jumped at the chance without hesitation and had lived and worked there ever since.

In the following years, Nicholas and Abraham became great friends...and whenever his father allowed him to tag along to John's Town, Nicholas was the first one ready to go. He knew full well that he would get to visit with ol' Abe again. It was always exciting to think about the stories Abe would tell. And there was always something different to hear.

***

As Manendra and Nicholas got off the horse and put it in the corral, the boy was thrilled to be going back to John's Town the next day to see the Major, but more importantly, to see his dear friend once again. It would be a bittersweet visit, though. Nicholas reckoned that they must have gotten news of his parents by now.

"Will I have to sleep right away, Uncle Joseph? I'm too excited and wide awake."

Manendra laughed and said, "Tonight, all of our people will be awake...young and old. You will know when it is time to rest. Now go, White Bear, and show your face around the fires. I will join you later...but remember," he warned, "do not speak in the English tongue...and if you are questioned about the color of your skin, tell them that Manendra is your guardian. They will know these words and will not challenge them."

With that, Nicholas nodded and headed directly toward the center of the village. He went up to the largest fire and saw the girl who had given him food the evening before sitting on a large blanket.

"Can I sit here?" Nicholas asked.

The girl flinched a bit from being startled and looked up. She saw that it was the English boy who had returned with her father. She quickly looked down, smiled, and nodded her head approvingly.

Nicholas sat down. For a brief moment they looked at each other, then smirked shyly in unison and looked away. Not long after, she made the first move to break the awkward silence.

"I am Tawanda."

Nicholas gazed upon her beauty, and as the light from the fire danced on her face, a strange emotion warmed his body. She looked back at him and laughed. Only then did Nicholas realize he was staring at her with his mouth half-open. He thought that he had better say something...and quick.

"I am...uh," he stammered.

"I *know* who you are, *White Bear*," she said, then sprang to her feet. "I'll be right back."

Nicholas felt dumb. He didn't suppose she would come back. He put his head down and wondered if he could ever get along with anyone in the village.

Moments later, he felt a light thud on the ground next to him and looked over to see Tawanda handing him a bowl of freshly cooked fish.

"Eat," she said, slightly embarrassed. "It is what you caught from the river today...and I cooked it for you not long ago!"

She looked down and waited patiently for him to taste it. But Nicholas was more intrigued by her beauty than by the meal. Tawanda giggled.

"It helps to put some in your mouth," she said in a motherly way.

Nicholas grinned and tasted the fish. "It's good...real good!" he said with a full mouth, and they both chuckled, which broke the ice completely.

Nicholas and Tawanda spent the entire evening together

talking, listening to some of the Indians who chanted to beating drums, and to the stories and tales of the elders. Nicholas didn't want it to end. He felt incredibly comfortable around Tawanda and she felt the same. But it did have to end, and when the moon was directly above them, and the fires were low, everyone retired to their shelters and sleeping blankets for the night.

Nicholas and Tawanda walked back to the longhouse together without saying a word. Inside, they stood next to Nicholas's blanket. Tawanda gave him a quick kiss on the cheek before scurrying away to her end of the longhouse. Nicholas was surprised by the sudden display of affection and sat down with his hand on his cheek. He lowered his head to rest and looked into the low burning coals. Whatever he was feeling earlier was now in the pit of his stomach, and in the center of his heart. And it was the last and most wonderful thing he felt just before he drifted into a deep, dreamless sleep.

Chapter VII

Nicholas awoke the next morning to find a thin coat, pants, and moccasins lying next to him. It was the finest set of Indian clothing he had ever seen, decorated with many symbols of the Mohawk. But there was one symbol that stood out from the others. It was the image of a walking bear, painted white. He thought that the artist had taken great care in designing the image.

Without further hesitation, he began to unbutton his cotton shirt to put on the new garments. Then he paused, his fingers still on the buttons. It was hard to let go of his past. His mother had made the shirt for him. She must have washed it a hundred or more times. He kept the shirt on and buttoned it up. From that day forward, he always wore a white cotton shirt under his Indian clothes.

Fully dressed in the Indian outfit, he rolled his stockings and shoes into his trousers and placed the bundle neatly under his blanket. He put his book there too, but kept in his waist, the knife his father intended him to have.

Nicholas stood up and felt a bit odd, almost as if he were wearing a costume. Yet the leather against his skin felt soft and smooth and was a perfect fit...as if it had been tailored exclusively to his size.

Glancing around the longhouse, he hoped that no one was watching him. And they weren't, as most of the dwellers were preoccupied with folding blankets and packing food and supplies for what he assumed would be the day's arduous trip.

He lumbered over to the fire pit, feeling a smidgen out of place, and helped himself to some breakfast. He ate while sitting next to the burning coals and, strangely enough, felt as if he were a part of something. It wasn't long before he became at ease in his new clothes and no longer had a feeling of estrangement. He started to feel like *White Bear*, and not so much more like *Nicholas.*

After breakfast, Nicholas knew what to do. He placed his bowl in the basket and hurried over to his bed. He took what was stowed under his blanket and rolled everything up together.

Outside, everyone was awake and moving about the village. The nine chiefs of the three clans led men on horseback into the woods, but most of the others followed on foot. He decided to walk with the men and boys, while the women and girls trailed behind.

To Nicholas's disbelief, a man shoved him and pointed toward the women.

"You walk with them!" he barked.

Nicholas stepped out of the line to fall behind. Some of the boys gave him hateful looks as they passed by. As much as he yearned to be accepted by the Indians, it seemed almost impossible because of the color of his skin. If he was going to remain with them, he had to prove, somehow, that he could be a part of their society.

He waited on the side of the trail for the women to catch up. When he saw Tawanda, he walked next to her. She looked at him in his new clothing and giggled.

"You look *very* brave, White Bear," she said, smiling.

"Thank you," he said, feeling a little sheepish, "I think." Then he choked out: "And you look good." He immediately wanted to kick himself for sounding childish, but Tawanda beamed at the compliment as she walked next to him.

It seemed like they walked a long distance, but Nicholas was too engrossed with Tawanda's company and beauty to care or notice. Nicholas discovered that Manendra was her father, and her mother was the woman who charged at him to leave the longhouse the morning before. Tawanda's mother had made his clothing, while Tawanda cut and stitched the pair of moccasins. She told him that his sleeping blanket had been used on a horse.

"That would explain the smell," Nicholas murmured to himself.

Tawanda said she was helping the other women make a new blanket for him, which made Nicholas feel honored that she had a part in it.

It was odd that he felt so close to her, since up to that point he had never really given girls much thought. But Tawanda was different. She paid him a lot of attention and seemed interested in what he had to say. He was growing very fond of her, and to him, it was becoming more than a "just friends" situation.

The Indian procession finally reached its destination, and even though Nicholas was excited about seeing the town and fort again, he felt distressed about leaving Tawanda's side. He wasn't sure when he would get another chance to be with her.

Everyone split into groups. The chiefs and their counselors separated from the other men while everyone else prepared to make a large camp. Nicholas went off by himself and headed straight for the stables.

Outside the barn, he saw a soldier conversing with a black man holding a team of horses hitched to a wagon. Nicholas kept his distance until the soldier went inside one of the blockhouses next to the manor. When the black man led the team into the barn, Nicholas ran over and looked inside.

"Abraham?" Nicholas shouted excitedly.

"Who's out yonda there?" came the familiar voice.

"It's me, Nicholas Dunne!" He stepped inside the barn. "My father is..." Then he caught himself.

"Say again?" hollered Abraham, stepping out from the shadows. "Ya gots to speak up a bit more, so's I can hear ya. Who'd you say it is?"

"It's me, Nicholas Dunne!" he yelled louder than before. "I'm the son of Patrick Dunne!"

"Patrick Dunne?" Abe responded in confusion, "I don' recollect no one by that name..."

Nicholas realized how long it had been since he saw his good friend. Abe must have been well into his seventies by now, and sadly losing his hearing...and possibly his wits.

"Hol' on now...let me see." Then it came to him. "My, my, my...Lawdy, Lawdy!" He quickly advanced toward Nicholas. "Nicholas Dunne!" he cried. "Git in here, boy, so's ole Abe can get a good look at ya!"

Abe looked a lot older than he remembered. His hair was completely white, his body quite thin and frail. His stoop was much more pronounced to the point that Nicholas thought Abe would lose his balance and fall.

"Hee, hee, hee...I'll be!" cackled Abe. "Well, you gonna stan' there all day lookin', or is you gonna meet me halfway...'cause I ain't as young as I looks any mo'!"

Nicholas sprinted over, threw his arms around him, and probably hugged him tighter than Abraham's fragile bones could stand. Yet the old man didn't seem to care.

"My, my, my...mmmm, mm," Abe said affectionately, pushing Nicholas away to get a better look. "If'n I should ever wonda, ye-ssa! Ye-ssa indeed! What have y'all been eatin' lately? Why, you musta growed at least three feet, I reckon'."

Nicholas grinned. "Still ain't taller than you, though."

"S'pose you're right about that," Abe agreed. "You's gettin' there. Tis' a fact! But 'nough about that. Let's go over yonda and set a spell, so's we can talk while ole Abe gets off'n these tired ole limbs o' his."

They walked a little further inside the barn and sat on two barrels under a window cluttered with cobwebs. Abraham had a thin cushion for his seat and let out a tired groan as he slowly sat down.

"Let me get my pipe goin'...then we can get to visitin' with one anotha." He crossed his legs and reached for the pipe perched on the dusty sill. "Now then, tell Abe what y'all been up to since the las' I saw ya'."

Nicholas assumed Abraham knew the fate of his parents, and was just being courteous not to mention it. So the boy started from the time they were last together. He told him about his homestead near the lakes of Garoga, how his mother taught him his lessons, and how he learned to speak the Mohawk language. He also reminisced about how wonderful things were with his parents and Indian friends.

All the while, Abraham barely said a word except for the occasional "mmmm, hmmm", as he puffed on his pipe. It wasn't until Nicholas told him of the recent frightful events that Abraham looked concerned. He let out a sigh, tapped the pipe against his shoe, and placed it back on the windowsill before standing up.

"There's somethin' you oughtta see," he said gravely, and led Nicholas to the far end of the barn. In one of the stalls was his father's horse.

"Major?" whispered Nicholas, wondering if it were really him and how he ever found his way to town.

48

Abraham cocked his head and leaned toward Nicholas. "What was that?"

Nicholas took a moment to reply, as he was admiring his father's horse. "Um, nothing. I'm just glad to see Major again!"

He supposed Abe bought the small fib, and luckily he was right. He didn't want to talk about it in case Abe didn't know exactly what happened, with Manendra and all. Instead, Nicholas rubbed Major's nose and thought that he was just as magnificent as ever. Just as much as the very first day his father brought him home.

***

Major Johnson had given the colt to his father as a gift some years ago for faithful service under his employment. At the time, Johnson told his father that the colt's lineage could be traced to the King of England's personal stock. His father was proud to have been honored with such a tremendous offering, and when the small brown horse was brought home, Nicholas was full of excitement.

Nicholas took great care of the animal and gave him his first name…*Patriot*. He didn't really know what the word meant and didn't care to ask. He had heard some men talk about "patriotism" and liked the sound of it. His mother and father didn't care for the name at all, although they never told him why, so they gave the horse a second name after its original owner.

Nicholas's parents made him swear that he would never call him "Patriot" unless he knew for certain that no one was around. The boy thought it was a bizarre request, but said he would be careful. Eventually he abandoned that name altogether.

"Someday he'll be put out to stud and you'll have a horse to call your own," his father told him one night in the barn. That was all the inspiration Nicholas needed to give a lot of attention to the farm's new addition.

***

Abraham explained to Nicholas that the frightened horse must have run away during the attack at their homestead and galloped back to Johnson Hall. Nicholas knew right away that it was Major he saw rushing past him in the woods when he was heading for the cabin.

"Found him that mornin' out on the lawn jus' outside…fillin' his belly," Abe said softly, gently petting the animal's broad neck. "Went up to him, and he almos' got away. He was scared somethin' awful! And when I sees the saddle, I knew right then and there who it belonged to, yessa. That's when I sent word to Major Johnson right away."

Abraham walked over to an old wagon next to Major's stall. "All that was with him, I kep' in here," he said.

Nicholas walked over and looked inside. They were his father's things alright; the saddle, pack, musket, and powder horn.

"Soon as Major Johnson got the word, he sent some men out lookin' for you an' your folk. But by the time they got to your place up in the hills, a bunch of Indians with that Manendra fella was already there."

Abraham walked away to give Nicholas some space and continued with his account.

"The Major was downright upset 'bout everythin', 'specially 'cause he wasn't tol' 'bout it till the next day when the soldiers came back. He knew right then that you was all right 'cause you was with Manendra, but in all my years, I don' recollect a time I ever did see the Major worry so."

A flood of sadness and despair consumed Nicholas as he ran his hand across his father's things. He felt like crying, but held back the tears, as he promised himself that he would never again lose control of his emotions again. Yet, every reminder of what had happened, was like a dagger in his heart.

Abraham's words seemed somewhat distant, until he patted Nicholas's arm and said, "Ya might wanna take a look in that pack. Major Johnson wanted everythin' left as it was."

Nicholas opened the pack and pulled out a satchel. Inside were some maps, a land deed, and a pouch filled with gold and silver coins. But that wasn't all. Lying in the bottom of the pack was a heart-shaped locket attached to a silver chain. Inside, was a small wisp of hair, and from the dark color he supposed it was his father's. The inscription inside confirmed his suspicion:

Cate,
To Keep With You While I'm Away –
All My Love,
Patrick

Nicholas closed the locket and placed it around his neck, tucking it between his jacket and shirt. He went over to his father's horse and gave him a rub on the nose.

"Thank you, Abraham, for keeping these things for me." He reached into the pouch filled with money and handed the old man a silver coin.

"Ain't no need for that, now," Abe said, taking Nicholas's hands in his. "Wouldn' be right with me, an' surely wouldn' be right with the Lawd. What y'all say we go see the Major now, hmm?"

Nicholas nodded his head. "Okay," he said.

They left the barn and slowly walked to the front of the house. Two guards stood at rigid attention at the top of the steep, wide steps that led to the manor's double entrance. They lifted their weapons and one of the men sternly commanded, "State your business!"

"Nicholas Dunne to sees the Major," replied Abraham.

"Step aside to the left," the guard ordered, then knocked on the heavy wooden door. Almost immediately a servant opened it and Nicholas and Abraham entered the main foyer.

"Please wait here," said the expressionless servant, closing the door behind them. He marched stiffly across the room and knocked twice on another door. He then entered and closed the door behind him. Within seconds the door flew open and Major Johnson ambled vigorously over to Nicholas.

"From the good of King George's grace, lad, it's true! You've been found and delivered to me from out of the wilderness!" The Major placed his hands on the boy's shoulders. "Are you well, my boy?"

Before Nicholas could answer, the Major continued, "Tsk, tsk, tsk. I desire nothing more than to never be plagued with such sleepless nights ever again! It's good to see that you're sound!" Getting down on one knee, the Major said with great sympathy, "I'm deeply sorry

51

for what has happened to your mother and father, Nicholas. They were two of the finest creations into which God ever breathed life. Please tell me that you still have your wits about you?"

"I am quite fine, sir," Nicholas assured him. "Manendra rescued me..."

"Yes, he did!" the Major interrupted excitedly and quickly rose. "Come with me, son." He placed a hand on the boy's back and gently pushed him forward. "There's someone here that I would like you to meet. Oh, and Abraham, a word with you this moment, if you will?"

Abraham bowed his head slightly. Turning back to Nicholas, Major Johnson said, "Wait here. This will only take a moment."

The Major walked over to Abraham and they went outside. Soon after, the Major returned alone and took Nicholas to his office.

In front of the Major's desk stood two men. One was Manendra, but the other was unfamiliar to Nicholas. He was well dressed, stood bold and straight with his arms crossed behind his back, and held the brim of his hat in his fingers. The two men watched Nicholas enter the room.

"Nicholas," said the Major, gesturing to the stranger, "this is Mr. Simmons."

The man slightly turned toward Nicholas and gave him a condescending glimpse.

"How do you do, boy," he said, showing an unnerving smile and bowing slightly.

Nicholas didn't quite reciprocate. Instead, he looked back to the Major with a perplexed stare.

"I have asked Mr. Simmons a favor regarding your best interests," Major Johnson said, standing formally behind his desk. "This gentleman is a business acquaintance of mine, and I know that this is a bit sudden, but he has assured me room and board as well as a proper education to fit your needs in these dire and tragic times. You would remain under his care until you are of an age to serve as an apprentice in his company."

The Major walked over to the boy and placed his hands on his shoulders. "You see, Nicholas, it's a chance for you to begin life anew...to become a fine young man, and to be respected throughout the community. Opportunities like these are seldom rendered, son, and because Mr. Simmons must depart within the hour, I'm afraid a swift decision must be made. So what do you say, lad?"

Nicholas felt his stomach drop. He looked at the stern, older gentleman and then to Manendra, who stood stiffly and without any expression. He looked back to the Major and said decisively, "With all due respect, sir, and without offending the charities of Mr. Simmons, who on your word *must* be a fine gentleman, I should like to decline the proposal for the time being...if it's okay with you, sir?"

Major Johnson placed his arms behind his back.

"I see...and what did you have in mind, Master Dunne?"

"I wish to stay with Manendra," Nicholas said, wondering if the request was a bit too presumptuous. Manendra gave no sign of acknowledging what he had just said. Looking back to the Major, Nicholas spoke confidently, trying to sound adult-like. "If it's okay with Manendra, of course, I think it would be best."

"Well then, gentlemen," the Major said, taking a deep breath and looking at the two men, "at the request of the young lad, I believe we are in need of some deliberating. Nicholas, if you would be so kind as to excuse us, I believe that Mr. Simmons, Manendra, and I have some details to work out. When we have reached a decision, I'll send word for you. Agreed?"

"Yes, sir," said Nicholas.

"Frederick will show you the way." The Major picked up a small brass bell from his desk and gave it a jingle.

The servant instantly opened the long paneled doors and entered the room.

"Nicholas, I will accompany you at a later time. And do me a great favor, will you," the Major said, putting on a pair of round spectacles before shuffling some papers on his desk, "get plenty to eat!"

"Yes sir," said Nicholas.

As he left with Frederick, he overheard the Major say to his companions, "Now there is a fine young man to be proud of. He acquires the exceptional traits of his dearly departed mother and father. Such a tragic ordeal, and may God shine his mercy on the poor, poor lad."

Chapter VIII

Nicholas found Abraham waiting at the foot of the porch steps. He held Major's reins and Nicholas noticed that the horse was outfitted with his father's things and ready to mount.

"All yours now," said Abraham, handing Nicholas the straps. "Is a fine, fine hoss, yessa, and can't say I don' disagree with Major Johnson when he says this ol' boy's gonna have a good home." He rubbed the horse's neck, looking into one of its large eyes.

Nicholas patted the horse's nose. "I'll take good care of him, Abe, I promise."

"Ain't no doubt you will...jus' as sure as there's rain."

Nicholas unbuckled the saddle, slid it off the horse's back, and held it out to Abraham.

"I want you to have this. I won't have any use for it, and it's what my father would have wanted. And it's what I want, because you've been such a kind friend."

Abraham looked at the saddle, as if thinking of refusing it.

"I'm sure it's worth a lot of money," Nicholas assured him, "and if you can't use it, I'm certain Major Johnson will take it off your hands."

"Don' go fussin' over ol' Abe, hear? I ain't got any need for no money, an' besides, think I might keep it a spell. Might make a good seat, too!"

Abe held the saddle before him, admiring it, and grinned at Nicholas.

Nicholas smiled back. He jumped up easily on the horse's back, something he had practiced quite often at home. When he was around nine, he'd balance himself on a woodpile to hop onto the back of one of their fidgety plow horses. The first time he did this his mother almost had a stroke and yelled at him to get down. His father was right on her heels, laughing so hard that Nicholas thought his sides would split.

That was the kind of trouble he got into. Nothing serious, yet

54

enough to nearly cause his mother to a faint at times.

Nicholas made himself as comfortable as anyone could get riding bareback, sitting tall while the spirited Major danced in a circle.

"Seems to be the perfect fit, yessa, Mr. Dunne," Abraham said with delight.

"I'd have to agree, Mr. Jackson."

"Don't forget to see ol' Abraham 'fore ya go now, hear?"

"You can count on it, sir," Nicholas said with a wave. As he left Abe behind with the saddle in his arms, an eerie feeling came over him. Almost as if that was the last real conversation they would ever have together. But he quickly fended off the notion and rode on.

Nicholas rode Major back toward the Indian encampment. The Indians turned to stare at him as he headed for the furthest part of the long, narrow lawn where the Turtle Clan was settled. Even though many of the Indian men didn't own a horse, he didn't feel the least bit apologetic to be riding Major. After all, it was the last great gift that his parents could have given him, even if it was made for him under the worst of circumstances.

He led his horse over to where the other animals were corralled and tied him to a tree. Boys were all around playing games and he decided to join them. He didn't feel like being alone and hoped that somebody would ask him about Major. Not for bragging rights, but just so he could talk to someone and maybe make a friend or two.

He saw Alok standing in a group and headed in their direction, but Alok moved away every time Nicholas got too close. He didn't understand why Alok was being so distant. He supposed it was because of his relationship with Manendra. If there were time later in the day, he wanted to talk to Alok and at least make another attempt to be his friend, if only for the sake of Manendra.

It was close to noon and Nicholas was getting hungry. Finding something to eat wasn't difficult, since there were many tables laden with an abundance of food prepared by the colonists and Indian people gathered on the vast grounds. Nicholas grabbed a plate and filled it with as much food as he could. He found a peaceful spot behind one of the blockhouses to eat in privacy.

Just as he was wiping his plate clean with some bread, Tawanda walked around the corner and sat next to him. Nicholas was glad to see her. She took the empty plate from him and placed it on the ground. Nicholas thought it both strange and confusing that she always seemed to be there for him, but he didn't question her about it. Nicholas wiped his hands on the grass.

"My brother is jealous of you, White Bear," she said while she pulled at some dandelions, her knees tucked up against her chest.

Nicholas gave her a confounded look. "Why me? I've done nothing to him...and I've tried to be friends with him, but he's the one that doesn't want any part of it! Why is he jealous?"

"Many reasons...to him anyway," she said. "He believes our father has given you all his attention ever since you've come to our village. The boys tease him and say harsh things to him because you are English. They know that Father has considered adopting you into our family."

"Does it bother you also?" Nicholas asked.

"It does not bother me at all!" she replied, with a little too much enthusiasm. "I like you because you are not like the others..."

Nicholas blushed. He never knew a girl to *like* him before. Where he was from, there were never any girls around to get to know, let alone like.

"...and I don't mind that I have to..." Tawanda continued, then broke off in mid-sentence.

"Have to what?" Nicholas probed, but she looked away and didn't respond.

"What?" he repeated.

"My father asked that I take care of you...at least until today...until he could speak to Major Johnson about what might become of you."

Now it made sense why Tawanda was giving him so much attention. He felt like an idiot for thinking that they might be closer than just friends. Nicholas felt betrayed by his emotions and let out a big sigh.

"But that's not why I do it!" she blurted, noticing his disappointment. "I do it because I want to!"

Nicholas felt that she was telling the truth, but that didn't stop him from wondering if their relationship would ever change to something more. Then again, maybe he was being a little self-centered because of everything he was going through. Maybe he was searching for something she couldn't give him. But he was growing impatient, and wanted to know how she felt about him regardless of her answer. Something in his life had to make sense. Otherwise, he thought he might go mad.

Nicholas was about to tell her how he felt when a muffled horn sounded from the vicinity of the immense lawn. Tawanda instantly sprang to her feet, scooped up his plate, and grabbed Nicholas's hand.

"Quick, get up!" she said excitedly. "The games are starting!" She darted forward, tugging on him to follow her.

"What games?" he said as he ran as fast he could to keep up.

"You'll see!"

When they reached the perimeter of the lawn, she finally let go of his hand and told him about the day's upcoming events.

"There are all sorts of games to compete in against the other boys. The winner of the most games receives a coat made of bear. There is a sack and foot race, a race on horseback..." She looked at Nicholas with wide eyes and yelped, "You can race your horse!"

Nicholas realized that she must have seen him on Major and he suddenly felt larger than life. Tawanda had been proud to see him go by, and some of the other Indian girls who knew that she was taking care of him had grown slightly envious. But that only made her more proud...and more loving toward him.

"Suppose I could," he said with a little uncertainty.

Another blow of the horn sounded.

"Hurry!" she pressed. "Go join the other boys for the foot race!"

Nicholas thought that it wouldn't be a bad idea. After all, he could run pretty fast, and he wanted nothing more than to impress her and show the other boys that he wasn't afraid to enter.

Without a second thought, he ran over to the starting line where the boys were already in position for the start. He could see a red pennant at the far end of the lawn marking the finish line. A man held a pistol straight in the air. Looking down the line of runners, he saw that there was another English-looking boy staring straight ahead and as still as a statue. Then the pistol went off. The other runners darted out in front to get the edge.

Halfway through the race, Nicholas had managed to get past all the other runners except for one...the English boy. He was much faster and Nicholas couldn't catch up to him. The boy flew past the finish line with Nicholas in second place, but it wasn't close. The crowd roared. Nicholas put his hands on his knees to catch his breath and watched the other runners cross the line. When Alok tied for fourth Nicholas felt a little sorry for him, because of what Tawanda had told him earlier.

Nicholas went over to the winner and shook the boy's hand. "You're pretty fast!" he said, still trying to catch his breath. "What's your name?"

"Andrew," he replied between short breaths. "Andrew Smith. Most folks just call me Andy. What's yours?"

"Nicholas Dunne."

The boy appeared to be somewhat taken aback by the name.

"You mean the *Dunnes* of Dunne's Flats in Garoga?" he asked with some concern. Nicholas lowered his head and nodded. He didn't realize that the news had spread so quickly.

"Oh," said Andrew. "Well, sorry about your folks and all, with what...you know...happened up there."

Nicholas kept his head down and nodded a second time. "Thanks," he said in a low voice.

"Well," said Andrew uneasily, "maybe I'll see you around." He gave Nicholas a quick pat on the arm. "Try the sack race later! I'll be your partner!"

"Thanks, but I think I'll just wait for the horse race."

"Suit yourself. See ya then, Nick!"

Another painful memory, because only his father ever called him Nick. But Andrew couldn't have known that, and it was still good to hear the name. He thought he might like to be friends with Andrew, not because they were both English, but because somebody his age (outside of Tawanda) didn't mind talking to him.

Nicholas watched as Andrew received a big hug from what were probably his parents. They were talking and laughing as they disappeared into the droves of people. It reminded him of the joyous times he shared with his parents. Another reminder of what should have been, but what would never be again.

Nicholas slowly walked back, wiping the sweat from his forehead. Tawanda was running toward him as fast as she could.

"White Bear!" she yelled, meeting up with him in the middle of the field. "Father wants to see you. He is up at the house with the Major. Go quickly!"

Nicholas knew why they wanted to see him and took off running. He hoped it was good news for a change.

Closing in on the house, he saw Manendra with Mr. Simmons and Major Johnson talking and shaking hands at the bottom of the steps. Mr. Simmons—the man he decided he really didn't like—climbed into a wagon, gave the reins a snap, and rode away. A bit of relief washed over Nicholas. It could only mean that he was to stay with Manendra. Or did it? His life had become as uncertain as the weather.

"Nicholas, my boy!" cried the Major at his approach. "It has come to a concordance that you will stay with Manendra and his people until he feels that you are ready to live on your own behalf."

The boy's heart soared. He looked at Manendra and saw the pleased look in his eyes.

"Are you willing to abide by the terms of this agreement?" the Major said, sticking out his hand, already knowing what the answer would be.

Nicholas grasped the Major's hand and shook it hard. "Yes sir!"

"Then, by the powers of His Majesty, your request is granted most humbly. Furthermore, let it be known from this day forward that you will keep in your sanctity the right to your Christian name, and also to be known as White Bear, noble and true member of the Mohawk Nation and of the Iroquois League. How say you, lad? Do we have an accord?"

"Yes sir!" Nicholas beamed shaking the Major's hand even harder. "And thank you most kindly, sir!"

There were so many things for Nicholas to be grateful for. He would stay with Manendra and be around Tawanda as much as he liked. He had a new home, and the struggles and pains of the past were starting to fade a bit. He would never be able to forget, but he had a chance to put some things to rest...or at least keep them tucked in the back of his mind.

Manendra put a hand on Nicholas's shoulder and said, "Go and join our people. I will find you in time."

Nicholas gladly obeyed and ran to find Tawanda to tell her the good news. He saw her petting his horse.

"Tawanda!" he yelled to her. "Tawanda, I'm going to..."

He stopped in mid-sentence the second he reached her. Nicholas saw that she was crying. He gently held her shoulders and turned her to face him.

"Tawanda, why are you crying? I can assure you that, whatever it is, we'll have plenty of time to talk about it when we get back home, and I swear..."

But he didn't get a chance to finish. She caught him off guard and flung her arms around him.

"I didn't know if I would ever see you again after today," she uttered. "I was trying to be happy for you no matter what might have..."

She couldn't go on. She was so relieved that she could only laugh in between tears.

Just then, a strange feeling came over Nicholas. For the first time in his life, he felt a love like no other. He *did* need her as much as she needed him. He didn't feel so much like a boy anymore. He felt more like...a man.

"It's okay, Tawanda," he said as lovingly as he could, not knowing what else to say or do. "It's okay," he repeated as he held her close.

Tawanda loosened her embrace on him, and thinking that they might have been seen, took a few steps back and wiped her eyes.

"I watched you race," she said in a shaky voice, still wiping her face. "You were very fast!"

"Not really," Nicholas said, a little disappointed. "I came in second."

"But you beat the Indian boys, and someday they will have great respect for you, I know it!"

Nicholas thought that she might be right. But it would take a lot more than a foot race to gain their respect.

"After the sack race is the horse race!" Tawanda reminded him.

"You must enter and get ready!"

He knew she was right. If he could win only one race, it had to be that one. Then he might gain their respect.

"Well, boy," said Nicholas, rubbing the horse's wide nose. "Are you ready? You can do it, fella. I just know you can!"

Nicholas looked around, and when he felt like no one was watching, gave Tawanda a quick hug. He hopped up on Major and Tawanda's face gleamed as she looked up at him.

"See you at the finish!" he said, lightly striking Major's hindquarter with the reins and giving him a quick jab with his heels.

The horse bolted with great speed, and as Nicholas gallantly rode off, Tawanda fell truly in love.

Chapter IX

Nicholas had all he could do to calm the high-spirited horse at the starting line. Major was nervous and excited when grouped next to the other horses. Nicholas rubbed his neck and whispered into his ear. It seemed to work a little, but not much. He hoped they would start the race before Major grew even more agitated.

The rules were simple...but not easy. Ride to the end of the lawn and onto the drive that encircled the property. There, the rider had to complete three full laps. Then, to finish the race, the jockey had to ride back to the lawn, race toward the house, and be the first to claim a hat that sat atop a pole. Only then would the judges declare a winner.

Nicholas was worried that it might be a tough win, since Major Johnson let some of the boys ride a dozen or so of his prized thoroughbreds. But unlike the footrace, this time Nicholas was ready. Leaning forward with his chest nearly on Major's neck, he waited for the crack of the pistol.

At the sound of the gun, Major bolted in front of the other horses. Nicholas could barely hold on. The tight group of competitors reached the edge of the lawn, where Nicholas used all his might to steer Major to the left and onto the road. Nicholas glanced back and saw that the other riders were at least three lengths back. He didn't have to do much to maintain Major's speed and made the three laps in no time.

As he neared the finish, he could hear the spectators' thunderous cheers over the hammering of the horse's hoofs and his own pounding heart.

Nicholas made it back to the edge of the lawn and rode as fast as he could toward the finish line. He'd never been on a horse with such a great speed, let alone the challenge of grabbing hold of a stationary object while at a full gallop. But he would give it his best no matter what happened.

The hat was within a few feet of Major's nose when Nicholas

stuck out his hand. With one calculated grab, he had it! But in the next instant he slipped off of Major's back and landed hard on the ground. It seemed like he rolled forever before he came to a complete stop. Major ran straight for the barn. Abraham yelled with horror from within as the animal nearly trampled him, and the audience howled with hysterics.

The other horses stampeded toward him and missed him by inches. No one knew if Nicholas had been trodden to pieces until the last of the horses flew past and the dust settled.

A deathly quiet fell as the crowd waited in anticipation to see if he was all right. Nicholas felt a great pain in his buttocks and lower right side. But the hat was still clutched in his hand, and he raised it to the sky. The crowd went wild. Some of the Indian men sauntered over to lift him from the ground and brush him off. One of them held up his arm and proclaimed, "He who dances with the earth is the victor!"

Everyone clapped and roared with delight, and even more so when the Indian's words were translated into English. Nicholas was glad that he could give everyone a good laugh, even if it was at his expense.

When everyone dispersed, Nicholas limped to a table to sit down. He grimaced as his bruised hindquarters touched the hard wood. It would be a few hours before he could join another event. The one he wouldn't miss for the world—which would grant him the most respect—was wrestling.

If Nicholas thought he could do anything well, it was hand-to-hand combat. From a very young age, Manendra had taught him how to handle an opponent to his advantage. It was how the Indian boys learned to prepare for the deadly art of warfare.

Manendra could be rough when training Nicholas, and one more thing that made his mother nervous whenever she watched from the cabin's doorway. But his father thought it was good for his son to learn how to protect himself...in case he ever ran into trouble in the wilderness.

"Let them be, Cate," he would say whenever she felt things were getting a little out of hand.

She was a very protective mother, but never once did she interfere. In her heart she knew that it *was* to his benefit to learn such valuable skills in order to become stronger and more independent. And even though Nicholas was thin and wiry, his muscles were hard from working around the farm, which enabled him to survive a throw or two from Manendra's strong arms.

Although quite sore, Nicholas was eager to show the Indians his wrestling talents. He wouldn't think of backing out now, and made sure he was the first to enter the contest. And he was.

The rules were explained. The contestants had to wrestle in as many matches as needed until only one boy was left. No one could carry any weapons on their person. If a weapon *was* exposed at any time during a match, the perpetrator would be immediately disqualified and his opponent declared the winner by default. The rules were that plain and simple, and yet could possibly get a little dangerous. That's why most of the boys from town were not allowed to participate. Their mothers wouldn't hear of it. But one English boy was allowed…and that was Andrew—the boy who won the footrace.

Nicholas's first opponent was easy. He had him pinned in a matter of seconds. But as he advanced through the matches, winning became more and more difficult. Yet, he won his first four matches, and the only other boys left in the contest were Nicholas and his next opponent, and Andrew Smith and his challenger.

Nicholas had watched Andrew wrestle and was greatly impressed. He was really good...maybe too good!

Nicholas's next rival was an Indian boy from the Wolf Clan. He was taller and a little bulkier than Nicholas, but that didn't bother him. After all, he had some tricks up his sleeve that Manendra taught him, which he was eager to show off.

The Indian boy immediately threw Nicholas to the ground and got on top of him. Nicholas winced when his injured side hit the hard ground. The boy had him in a headlock until Nicholas wrapped his legs around his head and twisted his body to throw him off. Both boys quickly sprang to their feet and circled one another.

The match had gone on for a few minutes and the Indian boy, who must have expected Nicholas to be an easy target, was getting quite frustrated. It didn't help when the men and boys of his tribe teased him for not taking Nicholas down so easily.

Because of the mocking, the boy erroneously lunged at his

opponent, but Nicholas stepped out of the way, kicked the boy's feet from underneath him, and then shoved him to the ground.

The Indian boy was stunned and noticed that all eyes were on him. Furious, he sprang up, pulled a knife, and went after Nicholas, slicing him twice on his arm. Even though the cuts were deep, Nicholas barely felt the blade touch his skin. Instead, he quickly grabbed the boy's arm and flung him to the ground. Nicholas threw himself on top of his opponent and wrestled the knife away from him. He pressed the point of the blade to the Indian boy's throat. The boy looked at Nicholas with shock and terror in his eyes.

Nicholas only saw an Indian under his blade—the Indian who murdered his father, and the one that scalped his mother. All recollections of that day came flooding back, like water flooding over a broken dam. His mind was now overflowing with hate. He wanted to kill him! He *needed* to kill him! He wanted to feel the knife plunge deep into his worthless neck. So deep that it would come out the other side and stick in the ground.

Nicholas gripped the knife with all his strength.

"*Nooo!*" came a shrill cry from the crowd. "White Bear! Please stop!"

Nicholas hesitated, and it was enough for Tawanda to act swiftly.

"No!" she screamed, and flung herself into Nicholas, knocking him on his side.

Nicholas was so taken back, he couldn't move. He looked at her and remembered where he was. He felt the pain in his arm, where the knife had sliced through the leather and into his flesh. He tossed the knife away and held his arm as he clambered to his feet. He pushed his way through the crowd and ran toward the lower end of the property.

Nicholas kept running until he found a stream just inside the woods. He dropped to his knees, took off his coat and shirt, and dipped his bloody arm into the cold water. After it started to numb a bit, Nicholas wrapped his shirt around the wound and sat on the bank. He could hear people cheering in the background as he sat alone. He tried to figure out why he had almost killed the Indian boy and felt deeply remorseful. Sadly, he realized that none of it was behind him. He had come so close to murdering another human being. That wasn't like him...*or was it?*

Nicholas heard shuffling leaves and jerked his head around. To his relief, he saw that it was Tawanda. She kneeled next to him, and without asking, cleaned the wound with water and applied some mud to cover the laceration. With a piece of cloth she made a temporary dressing.

When he had enough courage to speak, he murmured, "I'm sorry, Tawanda." She ignored him at first, focusing her attention on cleaning his bloodied shirt in the brook. Nicholas thought that it was better to keep still and not say another word.

She took Nicholas's hand and placed it on the bandage to hold it in place. She put her other hand under his chin.

"Look at me, White Bear," she said soothingly. "Do not be sorry for what happened...it is not your fault!"

Nicholas tried to look down, but again she lifted his chin to make him look at her.

"You have been through more than most will see in a lifetime, and you cannot control what has happened. But you *can* control the days that lie ahead in your future. You will have to find a way to put the things that upset you in a place that is not so easy to remember. Only then can your heart and mind be free...and only then will you find happiness once more."

Nicholas wanted nothing more than to do just that. He felt better just listening to her.

Tawanda stood up and brushed off her skirt. "Will you walk back with me?" she asked. "It will be dark soon, and I will worry if you stay here alone."

Nicholas nodded his head and pulled himself up. She looped her arm under his and they walked back toward the house. He didn't know if the people had forgotten about the dreadful incident, but he supposed he would find out soon enough.

Chapter X

Nicholas and Tawanda grew concerned when they reached the front lawn. Instead of everyone celebrating and enjoying the festivities, the people were quiet...too quiet. Groups of colonists and some Indian men were huddled near the bottom steps of the Major's house. Nicholas and Tawanda could sense the worry that filled the air and saw some of the Mohawk people quietly chanting and praying. Nicholas asked Tawanda to wait for him as he headed straight for the house. He joined some of the townsmen standing in a circle, so he could listen in on their conversations.

"Terrible news, it is," said one of the men.

"Things are going to change, I'm afraid," another man said worriedly. "Our future could be at stake, unless there's someone to lead us as *he* has in the past."

The men started to debate with one another, which became too confusing for Nicholas to understand. He quickly hailed a man passing by.

"Excuse me, sir!" said Nicholas. "What's going on? What happened?"

The man looked down at Nicholas as if he were speaking another language.

"Haven't you heard, my boy?"

Nicholas gave him a befuddled look.

"No, I don't suppose you have," he said gently, placing a hand on the boy's shoulder. "Major Johnson has just passed."

Nicholas gave him a blank stare. He barely heard the rest of grave news.

"Upstairs, in his bed," the man said, pointing to a second story window.

Nicholas was dumbfounded and stood motionless, staring up at the window. *Can't be,* he thought to himself. *I just talked to him only hours ago, and he was fine!*

For some reason, he immediately thought the Major might have been assassinated, perhaps poisoned or something. He bolted for the wide steps that led to the front doors.

When he reached the porch, the guards quickly lifted their muskets and blocked him so he couldn't pass. Without thinking, Nicholas tried to push his way through but was callously shoved back.

"I have to see the Major!" he cried, trying to force his way through a second time. Again the guards shoved him back, with enough force to deposit Nicholas on his tail end. He sat for a moment in a stupor. Not to be deterred, he got up and charged at them again with all his might.

"I have to see the Major!" he shouted.

Everyone within earshot was watching the commotion. Before the guards had the chance to throw him down again, an arm curled around Nicholas' mid-section.

"White Bear! Come!" Manendra said sternly, pulling him away. "It is time for us to join our people and pray for this great loss!"

With his head lowered and his fists clenched, Nicholas settled down a bit and tried to catch his breath. Manendra put an arm around his shoulders and led him away from the house. Nicholas turned his head around to give the guards a jeering stare, which they pretended not to notice. He knew they were just doing their job, but still, he hated them for it.

Manendra and Nicholas crossed the lawn and went to the south end of the grounds. Indians were erecting massive fire pits encircled with large stones, while others stacked large piles of wood next to each one. Nicholas assumed that a great ceremony of mourning was being prepared for the evening.

Manendra took him to their shelter and had him wait there until dark, while he went out to help the others. When evening came, Manendra stepped back inside and motioned for Nicholas to join him.

Outside, huge fires were burning so brightly that they lit the entire grounds. In the distance, huge shadows danced across the twin blockhouses, the stone fortifications that stood at each side of the manor. He thought he could make out some flickering candlelight in the tall, dark windows of the house.

Nicholas followed Manendra to one of the bonfires and was told to sit in a circle made up of at least fifty Indians. He scanned their faces to find Tawanda. It looked like she was sitting opposite from him, but he wasn't sure. The enormous fire blocked his view.

His arm ached. He saw a small patch of blood on his sleeve. The cut had opened up again. "All because of those damned guards!" he muttered.

Nicholas rarely cursed. His mother hated it, and now more than ever he tried to respect her wishes. He hoped that, wherever she was, she would understand.

The mood around the fire was quite serene and everyone appeared to be meditating. Then a band of Indian dancers entered the circle. They were dressed in colorful costumes adorned with beads, stone belts, earrings, and animal bone hanging from rawhide necklaces. Most had shaved the sides of their heads so that only a strip of spiked hair was visible, running from front to back. Some wore colorful feathers clasped to the hairs on the backs of their heads. Some had painted their scalps and faces with strange markings and symbols Nicholas had never seen before.

The beating of a nearby drum broke the quiet. It played for only a minute or two, but the echo eerily lingered on until it was drowned out by the crackle of the immense fire. Then the drumming started again. The dancers lightly skipped to the beat while slowly waving their hands in the air. There had to be at least twenty or so dancers. Strangely, though, no one voiced a sound, not even a whisper. Only one Indian sang to the beat of the drum, and just loud enough for everyone to hear.

Listening to the Indian chant, while watching the legs of the dancers split the light of the fire, Nicholas fell into a trance-like state. Again he felt alone, and it felt like he was plunging into great despair. Again and again, the reality of death plagued him. He didn't know how he could live through it.

Nicholas closed his eyes and tried to think of happier times. He had to do something for the sake of his sanity.

"White Bear," said a low, soft voice in his ear.

Nicholas opened his eyes and Tawanda was crouching next to him.

"It is late, and everyone has gone to sleep."

He looked around and saw that everyone *had* left. The once

ferocious fire was now a bed of red coals. He had fallen so deeply into his mournful thoughts that he didn't realize that he had been sitting alone for quite some time.

Tawanda held out her hand to help him up. "Are you all right?"

Nicholas rubbed his eyes and forehead. "I'm fine, just tired." He yawned and took her hand.

"I have made sleeping arrangements for you. We can speak in the morning, if you wish?"

Nicholas stood up and stretched his back. He wanted to talk to her, but was too exhausted to think about it, and the minute his head hit the ground, he was out.

***

"*Nicholas,*" said a familiar, soothing voice from the darkness. "*Nicholas, wake up!*"

Nicholas opened his eyes, but everything was blurry and distorted. He couldn't place it, but it seemed like he was standing at the edge of a forest near a place he once knew. When his eyes focused, he could see fire and thick smoke all around him. Human-like shadows danced within the white and gray plumes. He could hear faint screams coming from every direction, but he couldn't really make out anyone in particular. Then from the blazing inferno a white figure rapidly approached him, as if it were floating on air.

"*There you are, my prince,*" it said, hovering ten feet from him. "*I've been looking for you.*"

It was his mother! She floated slowly up and down and smiled at him. She wore a white gown soaked with blood to her waist. A hatchet was embedded in the side of her skull, and he could see part of her scalp, matted with hair and dried blood.

"*Help me, Nicholas!*" she pleaded, smiling deviously. She held open her arms and advanced forward to embrace him, but Nicholas backed away. She paused for a moment, still suspended in air, and the expression on her face became mean.

"*Why didn't you help your poor, dear mother, Nicholas? Why?*"

Nicholas was terrified!

70

"I wanted to, Mother," he choked out, "but I was afraid!" He dropped to his knees and looked up at her.

She placed her hands on her hips and slowly floated closer to him.

"*Tsk, tsk!*" she croaked horribly. "*Still trying to pull a fast one on me, are you?*" She bent over to put her face directly into his. "*Whatever will become of you?*"

She laughed shrilly, and as she did so, blood dripped from her mouth. She wriggled the hatchet free from her skull and held it high over Nicholas's head. He cowered and held up his hands to shield himself.

"NO, MOTHER!" he screamed. "PLEASE!"

***

Nicholas bolted up from his sleep and looked around. Everything was quiet...and everyone in the shelter was still asleep. He thought for sure that his pounding heart could have woken them. He felt it would pop right out of his chest.

He tried to keep silent as he gasped for air. Finally he was able to gather himself enough to lie back down. He pulled the blanket up to his neck while he stared up at the dwelling's coned roof. His head and chest were sopped with sweat, which chilled him to the bone.

For some reason he knew that it was hours before morning, but he couldn't get himself back to sleep. He tried to think of more pleasant things, like Tawanda. Thinking about her helped him to forget the horrific dream, and it seemed to work, because it wasn't much longer before his eyes closed once again.

In the morning Nicholas was the last one to rise. Oddly enough, he was quite rested. He went outside and found some food for breakfast, but didn't eat much. He overheard two of the natives in his clan say that there was going to be a short wake for the Major followed by a great funeral procession, and that everyone in the vicinity of the town was to attend. It wasn't something the Mohawk usually did for any Englishman, but Major Johnson was their ally. The people of the Iroquois had lost a good friend. More than that, they felt they had lost their only hope to live in peace with the white man, as the colonists were gobbling up their sacred lands.

Time and time again, Major Johnson would painstakingly defend the position of the Iroquois League. He tirelessly kept the Crown convinced that trade with the Indians was good for promoting growth and prosperity in the New America. Not to mention that there were thousands of Indians at their disposal who were willing to keep the French forces at bay. And any animosities between the colonists and the Iroquois would remain civil, just so long as the Indians were free to hunt and gather upon whatever lands they needed to live.

So, for the Major's good deeds, the Indians would pay their respects to him, even if it meant that they would be part of a traditional Christian service.

Later on, three uneventful days passed as the Major's body was prepared for the funeral. Nicholas kept to himself for the most part until the final day came to pass.

Nicholas saw Tawanda with the other women, but decided not to bother her. Instead, he met up with Manendra and was told that he, too, would represent the Turtle Clan in the funeral march.

"Our people will leave footprints in the ground," Manendra told him, "and follow the chief of many white men to the entrance where his fathers wait. This is to show the Spirit of Life, and the Spirit of Death, that the people of the Five Nations are not above the one who ascends to the skies. Today, he whose body returns to the earth from which he first came, and who is favored by the Gods, is above all men that are still living."

Nicholas understood what he meant. He also understood that he made a promise to Major Johnson before he died—to abide by Manendra at all times and to live by the ways of the Mohawk people. A promise he would never break, as if his life depended on it. It was something he learned from his father years ago. A man's worth was not weighed by gold, but by his words, and the actions created by those words.

That afternoon the Major's body was quietly removed from the house. His coffin was placed in a black carriage with windows decorated with fine etchings. The driver was also in black, sitting still and tall behind a team of four dark horses. Two footmen climbed aboard the back of the hearse.

Proudly waiting in front and in back of the black wagon was a slew of white warhorses that supported red-coated soldiers dressed in their finest glory. Behind them were the more prominent citizens, seated in day carriages and atop horses adorned with the finest of saddles and blankets. Everyone else would be the next in tow, and the Indian people would be the last to follow.

Nicholas got in line with the men and boys and, unlike the last time, was not forced to wait for the women. Everyone remained quiet as they waited for the procession to get underway.

The leading soldier of the caravan raised a sword and gave the order to proceed, and in unison, and as if already rehearsed, each group moved accordingly. Nicholas thought it was a very humbling event. The colonist's grim faces revealed that they took great care in giving the Major a proper farewell. He was loved and respected by all who knew him...and even by those who only knew *of* him.

Because the Indians were so far back, they would have to pass in front of the barn before reaching the left blockhouse. As they rounded the drive that led to the stable doors, Nicholas saw Abraham leaning over the side of a wagon, his pipe dangling from his mouth. When the carriage that transported the Major's body was out of sight, Abe entered the barn and closed the massive white doors behind him. Nicholas wondered what might become of him now that the Major was gone.

It didn't take long before rumors started to spread that the Major's young son—now a British officer stationed in England at the time of his father's death—was already en-route to make permanent quarters at his father's estate. The news did not sit well with the people of the small colony. Not in the least.

It was said that he was most unlike his father and not at all a friendly or lenient man, especially toward Indians. This was something the colonists worried about most. They feared an Indian uprising if more lands were taken from them, or if shady deals tricked them. No one could have known at the time that a great war would come, dividing the country between freedom fighters and loyalists. It would be a conflict that Nicholas would speak of in his later years as "a war of the Red Devil," and referring, of course, to the British Empire and not their Indian ally counterparts.

As they drew near the center of town and the church where the viewing was to take place, Nicholas couldn't believe his eyes. Thousands of people had come to pay their last respects to an honored man. He realized how fortunate he had been to know the Major and have the privilege of his company on many occasions. Nicholas never really knew how important he was, since he was a very down-to-earth individual who happened to bark out orders from time to time. He was as much of a family friend as any person he knew.

People lined the streets and crowded the church to get one final glimpse of the Major's body. Nicholas couldn't bear to see him in a morbid and artificial state, and decided to stay outside with some other boys and girls. He wanted to remember his friend as he was. He didn't think the Major would mind, since there was no intent to be disrespectful.

Nicholas sat alone and thought about the last time he saw the Major, alive and well, just days before. Even though he felt that Manendra would take good care of him, he was a little worried that his only other safe haven was gone. He still had to consider the possibility that he might have to take care of himself, although hopefully not for at least a few more years.

Tawanda stayed behind as well. The wake wasn't something that interested her either. Though, as soon as she caught up with Nicholas, she did tell him that Alok and some other boys were practically trying to claw their way inside the church to see the Major's body. The whole thing disgusted her, and Nicholas thought they were no better than a swarm of vultures. Yet, all he cared about at the moment, was that it was a beautiful, sunny day for his dearly departed friend, and that Tawanda was there to help him get through his mourning.

They sat and talked for a long time, and Nicholas learned many things about her. He realized he had no doubt about his love for her, and would somehow find a way to never be without her. She was a part of him...a part of his heart that couldn't be replaced if it ever went missing.

The viewing hours finally ended and everyone inside the church gathered on the main street of town. The carriage carried the Major's body to the cemetery for burial. And at the final resting place, the local minister spoke a short sermon and the casket was lowered into the ground. Before the first spade of dirt was thrown into the grave, everyone departed and went their separate ways.

Nicholas walked back to Johnson Hall with his clan, where everyone gathered up their things and prepared for the journey home. There was no point in staying. Any talks that the Major intended to have with the Iroquois were now indefinitely postponed.

Before leaving, Nicholas had time to go to the barn to see Abraham. He found him sitting sideways on the saddle that Nicholas had given him, which Abraham had placed atop the barrel next to the window. His pipe lay unlit on the sill as he looked beyond the webbed and dirt-stained glass. He had hardly noticed that Nicholas had taken a seat across from him.

"Lawd, Lawd, Lawdy," he muttered, shaking his head and rubbing his temple. "Tis' a sad time to be in the worl'. Don' knows what I'll do now."

"I miss him already," Nicholas said with a heavy heart, hoping that Abraham wouldn't feel so alone.

Trying to lighten the conversation, Abraham tapped on the boy's knee with his knuckles and said reassuringly, "Well now, Mr. Nicholas, don' you worry 'bout none o' that. You's gonna be jus' fine. Ol' Abe knows it for a fact, yessa."

"What are you gonna do now, Abe?" Nicholas asked with great concern.

Abraham thought for a moment, then looked back to the window. "Reckon' I'm jus' gonna stay put for the time bein'. Don't know anythin' else. But, don' be worryin' 'bout me," he said, getting up with a groan. "You got yourself to look after."

Nicholas couldn't help but feel sorry for him. Abe looked like he had aged ten years since the day he last spoke with him. He saw Abe's hands tremble and wished there was something he could do for him. Although, he had a hard time taking care of himself.

"You best be goin', son, 'cause I'm shore that they's waitin' on ya. Besides, I'm thinkin' that I might need a little time to myself," he said, holding out one of his hands. "Don' forget to come back and see ol' Abe when you can now, hear?"

Nicholas stood and gave him a giant hug.

"Lawd, dear Lawd," Abe murmured, as a tear fell from his eye.

Nicholas let him go and ran from the barn. He thought for sure that he would lose his emotions right then and there, but crying seemed like too much of a childish a thing for him to do anymore. Besides, he didn't want the others to see him in a moment of weakness. Instead, he went to his horse to be alone...just in case he did break down. When it was time to leave, Nicholas was glad to be going. The sooner he could put the day behind him, the better.

On the way back to the village, each clan of the Mohawk parted ways and headed south, while the rest of the Five Nation tribes took a route to the west, following the Great River. Nicholas never again saw the boy who cut his arm. And that was just fine with him. He did hear, however, that the English boy Andrew Smith, won most of the contests and was declared champion of the games. Major Johnson personally awarded him the bear coat trophy, shortly before he fell ill and died.

It was nearing dark by the time Nicholas could see the river through the trees. The light of the disappearing sun reflected off the rippling waters. Nicholas was relieved to be back in his new home.

But, he wondered, *what would happen next?*

He hoped nothing, but his gut told him he was probably hoping for too much.

Chapter XI

It didn't take long for Nicholas to settle into his new life with the Mohawk people, and even though it had only been two months since his parents had died, the mental suffering was somewhat fading.

To help pass the time, he learned all he could about the Indians and their way of life. He was so busy during the day that it helped keep his thoughts at bay. The nights were different, though. He was still plagued by nightmares. Some were worse than others. Over and over he would wake up soaked with sweat, his heart pounding in the darkness with no one there to comfort him.

The mornings were always a thankful relief. He would get dressed, have some breakfast, and go out to mingle with the other boys, or venture out on his own to explore the immense wilderness. Of course, there were always chores to take care of first—collecting firewood and gathering food and water. The women and younger children did most of this work, though. Boys his age spent most of their spare time learning how to use weaponry and other hunting and warrior skills. Any time left could be utilized for basket weaving, leather crafting, and canoe building…all things that Nicholas loved to do. Outdoor activities came naturally to him, as they did for his father. Hunting and trapping were his favorites. He liked the challenge and skill required to stalk and capture game, and he was becoming very good at it.

The boys were not yet allowed to hunt big game like deer or the occasional moose or bear, but they were allowed to hunt and trap all sorts of smaller game, like waterfowl, rabbit, fox, beaver, or even coyote. It wasn't unusual for Nicholas to bring back a rabbit or two or a few squirrels. Anything he captured or killed was used with little or no waste. The meat was shared and used for sustenance, hides were separated for leather products, bones would be fashioned into cooking utensils, and organs were sewn to make pouches. Even feathers, claws, and other parts of the animal were used as jewelry or decorative items.

Two of Nicholas's proudest catches were a raccoon and a red

fox. He made a winter hat from the raccoon's pelt—its face for the front and its tail for the back—and from the hide of the fox he fashioned a sling for his musket, though he was seldom allowed to use the firearm. He thought his father would have been proud of his work.

The furry, reddish-orange sling was a handsome addition to the gun, and Nicholas cared well for both items. He kept them clean and waterproof by applying animal oil to the sling and to all parts of the gun. He knew that he would use it someday soon, when the braves taught the boys to hunt big game with both bow and musket.

Primarily, the bow was used more often, since it was more economical to make arrows than to trade goods for gunpowder and ammunition. Nicholas loved the challenge of making his own bow and set of arrows for small game hunting, and couldn't wait to try them out. His first hunt for small game didn't go as he planned. Then again, nothing else in his life did anyway.

His first kill was a young button-buck. Creeping through the woods, he came upon the animal by chance. His heart pounded in his eardrums. He crouched behind a tree and peeked at the young deer which drank peacefully from a slow moving brook. Carefully, Nicholas reached behind to grab an arrow from his quiver and quietly cradled it on the bow. He pulled the arrow back as far as he could and aimed for the heart behind the lower part of the shoulder. His arms began to tremble.

The deer raised its head and looked straight at him. They stared at each other for a long moment, until Nicholas thought that the staring contest had gone on long enough.

He took a deep breath, held it, steadied himself, and let the arrow fly. It punctured the animal's side almost exactly where he aimed. The stunned buck kicked up its hind legs and bolted in the opposite direction. Nicholas didn't move. He watched the animal zigzag through the trees and disappear into the woods, its white tail pointed straight up. He remembered to keep track of what direction it was headed. Even a direct hit through the heart wouldn't put the beast down, as its adrenaline would keep it running.

Nicholas walked the twenty yards to where the buck had been hit. There were no signs of blood, only deep hoof marks left behind in the soft ground.

He followed the tracks until he noticed small droplets of blood. He found more blood the further he advanced, and eventually discovered the deer lying helplessly on the cold, wet ground behind a large boulder. Eyes wide with dread, it gasped for air. The arrow appeared to have sliced through its lungs instead of the heart.

He felt sorry for the animal as its upper body heaved, trying to find a last breath or two. He almost felt as if he had committed a great sin, though he would make sure that all parts of the carcass would be used with great care.

Soon after the deer expired, Nicholas took the knife from his belt, and as he was taught to do so, cut through the thick skin of the underbelly to remove the entrails. The heart was still warm and completely unscathed. Holding it up to the heavens, he said a prayer of thanks and got right to work. He would have to get the remains back to the village by himself, and anticipating how proud Manendra might be, he found the strength to drag it out of the woods and back to camp.

Manendra was admiring a large beaver that Alok had trapped when Nicholas appeared, dragging the deer behind him. Men and boys went over to help, and Manendra joined them. Alok was annoyed that his father was once again paying more attention to Nicholas. If Alok caught one fish, Nicholas would catch three. If he trapped a rabbit, Nicholas would trap a fox...and now a beaver, for a deer. He was jealous, even angry, to the point where he started to hate the English boy.

Alok angrily took his beaver to their longhouse, ignoring the great fuss made over Nicholas.

Manendra knelt down to take a closer look at the deer.

"It is a fine buck...and now you know the meaning of life and death as the Kanien-ke-ha-ka' do," he said, looking up at Nicholas who was still trying to catch his breath. As the men and boys admired the small deer, Manendra declared, "White Bear has learned that the arrow is swift, and that his brother is vulnerable. And so, the time has come. White Bear is granted the right to learn the skills of the warrior."

The men let out great whoops, and Nicholas felt this was the proudest day of his life. Some of the men carried the deer back to the longhouse so Nicholas could finish dressing and preparing it.

Everyone would share the meat, but the hide was his to do with as he pleased. Nicholas thought he would make a new pair of leather trousers, and hand down the leggings that were first given to him. He couldn't wait to get his next deer so that he could fashion a new jacket for himself. Mostly, he wanted to make something for Tawanda...a gift for being there for him in his time of need. He would make her a new pair of moccasins, or maybe a belt and necklace...something to show her how much he thought of her.

Everyone in the village knew that Nicholas and Tawanda were close. Even Manendra couldn't help but notice that his adopted son intrigued his only daughter. He was afraid that she was getting too infatuated and hoped they wouldn't be foolish enough to run off together. Manendra put trust in the fact that they would have enough sense to be properly married and become a permanent fixture in the longhouse. After all, they were still too young to make such decisions on their own, and there was still so much for both of them to learn.

Alok also saw that his sister was getting too serious. He tried to talk to her but it was useless. Tawanda couldn't understand why her brother was being so protective of her. What she didn't realize was that Alok was trying to coax her away from Nicholas because of his own personal vendettas. Their attraction to each other bothered him like a deeply buried splinter. He wanted to be rid of Nicholas once and for all before his whole family was infected.

The first step was to befriend Nicholas and pretend to want his attention. It wouldn't be hard. Nicholas had yearned to be friends with Alok ever since Manendra brought him to the village. So instead of avoiding Nicholas, Alok would do just the opposite to gain his trust...a trust that would fall perfectly in line with his plans.

Meanwhile, Nicholas made a gift for Tawanda and presented it to her when they were alone. She opened the wrapping of thin deer hide and smiled when she saw a leather belt and necklace made with quartz stone and antler bone.

"These are the most beautiful things I have ever seen, White Bear!" she said, giving him a giant hug. "I will be honored to wear them!"

Nicholas felt himself blush. He was relieved to see how much she enjoyed the gifts. From that time forward, she was sort of *his* girl, and his motive may have been just that—to show the other boys that she was already spoken for and that they shouldn't get too close to her. But after the boys saw what Nicholas did to the unfortunate wrestler from the Wolf Clan, they thought it better to steer clear of him. Some of them even whispered behind his back that he might be a little crazy.

After seeing the gifts that Nicholas gave to Tawanda, Alok found the perfect moment to befriend him. He searched the camp and found him grooming Major.

"Your pony is fast," Alok said, patting the horse's shoulder.

Nicholas looked at him for a brief puzzling moment without comment and went back to brushing Major. He thought it strange that Alok would approach him, after ignoring him on every occasion since his arrival.

"I saw the things that you gave to my sister. They are nice," he said, as sincerely as he could bear. "Did you make the belt from the deer you killed?"

Nicholas couldn't contain himself anymore. Thinking that Alok was up to no good, he looked at him and said, "Why are you trying to be friendly with me? You have kept your distance ever since I came to the village. I don't understand."

"I thought you were different," Alok said, "but now I see how kind you have been to Tawanda. I was only trying to protect her."

"Oh," said Nicholas, still not convinced, and went back to brushing Major.

"I thought that since we are brothers now, we should be friends and look out for one another. But if you don't want to," Alok said with a shrug, "then I'll leave you alone." He turned and started to walk away.

Nicholas was still confused, but thought it would be better to make friends with him now and worry about the details later. Besides, Alok *did* approach him first, and he knew that Manendra would be happy if they could put their differences behind them. Something still bothered him, though, and he couldn't figure out what it was.

Nicholas turned to him and said, "If you really want to be friends, then I'm glad."

Alok stopped and formed a devilish grin. Then he wiped the smile from his face, turned around to face Nicholas, and said, "Do you

81

want to go trapping? I've made a new foot-sling, but I haven't tried it out yet and thought that you might want to help me with it."

"Sure!" said Nicholas with a bit of enthusiasm. "Let me get some things and I'll meet you at the trail."

Alok turned away and smiled again. "Fool!" he said to himself before running to the longhouse to gather his own things.

Nicholas was still confused by the sudden act of kindness, but he couldn't resist trapping. He left Major alone to graze while he went to get his gear.

Nicholas had a good time with Alok, and he was happy to have a new companion. And from that time forward, and all throughout the winter months, the boys would hunt, trap, and fish together. They shared their catches with each other and became very close. Manendra was greatly pleased to see them enjoying each other's company. Tawanda, on the other hand, was not so sure about the new allegiance. She knew her brother well enough to be suspicious of such a quick change and remained that way until the following spring. Tawanda didn't tell Nicholas how she felt because, if Alok's intentions were truly genuine, there was no reason for her to interfere. But that all changed when she inadvertently overheard Alok speaking to some of the other boys from behind a hut.

"He thinks that he is better than me," she heard Alok say in a muffled voice, quite unaware that his sister was listening in on the conversation. "I'll show him, and soon he will know not to mess with me!"

Tawanda ran and found Nicholas sitting next to the longhouse, fashioning some hide into leather strips. She told him what she had heard, but Nicholas wasn't convinced.

"Did he mention my name?" he said, carrying on with his work.

"No, but he must have been talking about you," she pressed. "You are the only one who has ever made him jealous. Before you came to the village, he was better at everything than the other boys. I do not trust him and it makes me worry!"

"Aw, you're just being suspicious, Tawanda. He's been a good friend for months now," he said, smiling at her, "and we've been doing everything together. Besides, he has nothing to worry about. He knows that I wouldn't do anything to embarrass him in front of the others."

Tawanda decided to abandon the issue, but not before getting in the last say. "Just be careful, Nicholas," she pleaded, holding his arm. "He may be up to no good, but I hope I'm wrong!" Then she left him alone.

"Odd," Nicholas thought. "She's never called me by my given name before." But he quickly forgot about it and focused his attention back on his work.

Later on, he surmised that Tawanda was being a bit too cautious. And he and Alok continued to do things together, and had much fun doing it. So much so, that Alok himself started to feel like he would *miss* their times together in the woods and at the river.

Chapter XII

During the next new spring, Nicholas was sound asleep in the very early morning hours when a couple of taps to his head stirred him awake. Alok was squatting next to him.

"Alok, what is it?" he said groggily, perching himself on his forearm.

"Let's go!" he whispered.

"Go where?" Nicholas said, rubbing his eyes.

"Fishing!" he said excitedly. "What else?"

"Fishing," Nicholas repeated, looking around the dim quarters. "What do you mean, fishing?"

"Fishing!" Alok said with quiet exuberance, trying not to wake the others. "I have a canoe ready! Get your things and meet me down by the river bank!" He walked lightly to the entrance of the longhouse.

"Alok, wait!" said Nicholas as softly as he could, but Alok kept going without turning back. Nicholas grabbed his clothes and fishing gear and followed after him.

Outside it was still dark. The moon was gone and there was a vague hint that the sun would creep over the horizon within the hour. Nicholas was trying to put on his moccasins and head for the river at the same time. He finally caught up with his friend at the river's edge, where he saw a canoe halfway in the water with Alok's gear inside.

"What are you doing?" Nicholas asked. "It's too dark and dangerous to fish, not to mention that the river is moving too fast! If Father finds out about this, he will get angry with us!"

"Don't worry," Alok said with confidence. "I've made an anchor to keep us from floating too far downstream. By morning everyone will see how much fish we have caught, and they will praise us for it, unless…you're too afraid to go," he challenged. "If so, then I will go by myself and be the brave and honorable one." Alok knelt in the canoe and took up a paddle.

Nicholas looked at the fast moving water and didn't feel any more comfortable with the crazy idea.

"Let's just wait until everyone is up. Then we will know if it's okay to go on our own!"

"You know that Father won't let us go," Alok charged. "This is our chance to prove to him that we are not boys anymore, and that we can take care of ourselves."

"I don't know," Nicholas said with skepticism.

"If you don't want to go, then fine," Alok huffed. "I will go by myself." He started to set himself adrift from the sandy shore.

Nicholas grabbed the canoe to keep it from going any further. "Alok, you can't paddle the currents by yourself! It's impossible!"

"Then go with me! I promise that we'll stay close to the shore. Otherwise, step back!"

Nicholas sighed in defeat, and reluctantly stepped into the canoe. "All right...but I'm taking the back, so turn around!"

"Fine," smirked Alok, as he positioned himself to lead the front of the canoe.

The boys took their paddles, dug them into the soft sand, and shoved off. At first Alok kept within a few feet of the shore. The water was rushing so fiercely that Nicholas could barely hear Alok speak.

"Just a little further out and I'll drop the anchor!" Alok shouted back.

"What?" yelled Nicholas, but Alok didn't hear him. Alok deliberately paddled the canoe farther from the river's edge. Nicholas grew alarmed and tried with all his might to counter the course that Alok was hell-bent on keeping.

"What are you doing?" Nicholas screamed, but Alok either couldn't hear him or was plainly ignoring him.

Finally, to Nicholas's relief, Alok pulled in his paddle and threw out a large rock secured with rope, anchoring them near a point of land that jutted from the shoreline. Alok's smile made Nicholas very uneasy.

"Throw your line near the shore," Alok yelled, pointing to calmer water near the rocky shoreline. "The largest of the fish will be hiding on the bottom to keep away from the current!"

Nicholas did as he was instructed, even though he still thought the whole idea was completely insane. The only reason why he went along on the trip was because Alok seemed foolish enough to try the escapade by himself. He should have tried harder to talk him out of such a dumb thing. They might catch a lot of fish, but could be killed in the process of doing so.

Just as Nicholas was starting to feel slightly comfortable in the rocking canoe, Alok pulled out a knife, cut the anchor's rope, and yelled, "Have a good journey, *White Bear*!" Before Nicholas could react, Alok stood up and dove into the calm water close to shore.

The canoe almost tipped over and was quickly swept up into the pounding current. Nicholas grabbed a paddle and tried to make it to the shore, but the canoe smashed into a log, tossing Nicholas into the frigid water. As he came up, the log jammed him into a boulder jutting out from the rocky point. One of the branches nearly pierced his skull as he reached for a small hemlock that grew in between the rocks. Nicholas pulled himself out of the water and, in doing so, a splintered branch gashed his leg

"Aaaah!" he screamed in pain.

Nicholas lay on a large, flat rock holding his leg. He pulled up his leather pants and saw a neatly split gash in his flesh. He almost fainted. Then he heard a barely audible voice over the rushing waters.

"Help me!"

Nicholas couldn't see anyone, but knew it must be Alok.

"Help me!" came another faint cry.

Nicholas saw Alok gripping a log that dipped and bobbed in the raging current. He violently thrashed his arms to keep from being pulled under.

Nicholas painfully turned on one knee and slithered over the rock toward Alok. The cold spray of the water helped numb his leg as he inched his way out further and onto the log. He was close enough to see that a branch protruding from the tree had ripped through Alok's shirt, holding him hostage. Alok was trying to take deep breaths before the log thrust him under repeatedly. The log could give way at any moment and sweep them both down river.

Inching forward, he grabbed Alok by his shirt and somehow pulled him up and over the branch.

"Hold onto the log and try to make it toward the shore!" Nicholas shouted.

They inched their way backward until they finally reached the rocky shore. Just as Alok clambered half-way onto the stones, the log gave way with a loud crack and he lost his footing. Nicholas grabbed Alok by the arm and pulled him to safety…with not a second to spare. The log bobbed into the rushing water and quickly sunk. They climbed the rocky bank to safety and collapsed.

Trembling from the cold, they lay there trying to catch their breath. Finally Nicholas sat up, took hold of Alok's shirt, and pulled him close.

"Never come near me again!" he warned. "If you do, I swear I'll kill you!" Then, as hard as he could, he shoved Alok back to the ground.

Nicholas got to his feet and limped back toward the village. Alok sat up, waited until Nicholas was out of sight, and then trailed behind him, being careful not to follow too closely. He was able to skirt around him and make it back to the village first. Alok sat next to a small cooking fire to get warm. Nicholas wasn't far behind, and when he arrived, plopped his body on the opposite side of the fire. Some of Indians looked at the drenched pair with curiosity while they made their morning preparations.

Manendra appeared from the longhouse and approached the fire.

"Why are my sons wet and bruised?" he queried, waiting for a response with his arms crossed. "There is a canoe missing from the river's bank, and you do not have one with you. Tell me why I am questioning these things."

Both boys put their heads down.

Manendra grew impatient.

"Alok? White Bear?" he said sternly. "What is the truth that you are hiding from me? Speak!"

Nicholas raised his head. "We went to fish, Father. We wanted to surprise everyone with a great catch, so that we might be praised."

Alok looked at Nicholas in astonishment.

"We hoped that you would be proud of us, but instead we have made you angry." Nicholas continued, not knowing if Manendra believed him or not.

"A great log hit our boat and sent us into the fast moving water. We were able to save ourselves, but everything else was lost."

Although Nicholas didn't tell the whole truth, he thought he might have convinced Manendra. He knew what Alok had tried to do, but if he told the truth, Manendra would be furious. He wouldn't understand why Alok would attempt such a thing, since the two of them had been so close in the past months. Furthermore, Manendra might think he was lying to save his own neck from being scolded.

Alok lowered his head, waiting for Manendra to harshly discipline them. He didn't understand why Nicholas wasn't telling the whole truth.

"Dry yourselves and tend to your wounds. When you are finished, you will come to me in the longhouse," he ordered. "Then I will decide what your punishment will be."

Before he left, he gave them an abrasive look and said, "I will not wait long for you. If I do, my judgment against your actions will be more severe." Then he left them to think about his words.

Alok looked at Nicholas, but he was too busy inspecting his leg. And after he dried off a bit, Nicholas looked for Tawanda to help him stitch and bandage the wound.

He found her helping the other women, who were getting ready to go out and gather berries, roots, and other staples.

Tawanda led him to a blanket and helped him sit. She left him for a brief moment and soon returned with herbal remedies, stitching, and strips of cloth. Nicholas groaned as he pulled up his leather pant leg to expose the wound.

"Sit back," she said, covering him with a blanket and forcing his hands away from the gash. "Bite on this."

She gave him a strip of leather to put between his teeth. Nicholas groaned some more as she cut away the dead skin and lathered it with a stinging concoction. Then, she skillfully sewed the wound shut.

"What happened?" she asked, cutting the thread. "I overheard Father say that you and Alok went fishing and had an accident. But it was no accident...was it?"

"It doesn't matter," Nicholas said through clenched teeth.

"It matters to me!" Tawanda retorted. "I was right when I said he would be up to no good. What is the truth, White Bear? Tell me!"

Nicholas tried to convince her that it was just an accident, but he knew she didn't believe him. Not wanting to lie to her, he reluctantly told the whole story as long as she promised not to tell Manendra. But after hearing what her brother tried to do, she wouldn't let the matter go and decided that something should be done without Nicholas knowing about it.

Nicholas squeezed Tawanda's hand as she helped him up. He went into the longhouse to find Manendra and Alok sitting around a fire pit. He sat down and waited for Manendra to speak.

"You did not commit a crime for wanting to fish in the Great River," began Manendra. "Your crime is that you took a canoe and put yourselves in a dangerous path. You did not get my permission, and you failed to learn from all that has been taught to you." He looked at them and continued in a calm voice. "When you disobey, there must be punishment to teach you what is right, and what is wrong. How can either of you expect to become a warrior of the Turtle by making foolish mistakes? Yet, because my sons have committed only this one offense, I have decided to be more lenient with the punishment."

Nicholas and Alok felt relieved. Although Nicholas was still upset with himself for not telling his step-father the whole truth, he knew by doing so, it would only make matters worse.

"Neither of you will hunt, trap, or fish. Neither of you will be able to join the other boys to learn the ways of the warrior until I have decided that a lesson has been learned. You have embarrassed our people and your punishment has been decided."

Manendra wouldn't look at either of them as he handed down their sentence.

"You will only gather what needs to be gathered with the women and children. You will do as the women tell you, and you will do these things until you remember the right way. I will let you know when you are ready to re-join the men and boys." He thumped his chest with his fist. "Only then will my sons be ready to learn again. Now go!" He dismissed them with a motion of his hand.

Nicholas and Alok immediately left Manendra and went to the women to carry out their punishment. The rest of that spring and well into the summer, they worked alongside them. The other boys laughed and scoffed, and threw stones at them as they went out to work. It was humiliating, but for Nicholas the hardest part of all was not being able to hunt and trap.

As the months passed, Manendra felt they had been punished enough and let them rejoin the others.

The two boys never did do anything together again. Tawanda saw to that. She made sure her brother kept his distance from Nicholas, even though Nicholas wanted nothing to do with him. Alok was still jealous and spiteful, even though Nicholas had saved his life. Nicholas was still getting all the attention and the other boys rubbed Alok's nose in it. He thought more than once about getting rid of Nicholas another way, until one fateful night finally convinced him otherwise.

A few weeks after the incident, Tawanda quietly rose from her bed, so as to not awake the others. She grabbed her gathering basket and stepped lightly into the night. At the river's edge, she filled the basket with heavy stones and slung it over her back. She crept back into the longhouse with the hefty pack and went over to where Alok was sleeping. She sat on his chest and pinned his arms under her knees. Alok awoke with a start, only to find that he couldn't move under the enormous weight. Tawanda had a tight grasp of his hair and held a knife to his neck. Alok's eyes bulged with fear as he looked up at her.

"Tell me, *my brother*," she snarled, glaring at him as he tried in vain to wriggle free, "why I should not open your throat and let your blood spill into your bed? I know what happened at the river. I heard you talking to the others before you decided to be his *friend*," she hissed. "But don't worry. I will not tell Father what you did. But I will tell you this—stay away from him, and you won't have to keep an eye in the back of your head!" she advised, and yanked his hair. "If you ever go near him again, I will not be so forgiving the next time!"

Tawanda shook him to make sure he understood and warned him one last time through clenched teeth, "Do you hear me with your ears, *my brother*?"

Alok nodded as she pressed the sharp blade close to his skin. Tawanda slowly released him from her grip. She got up and tossed the knife alongside his head as a final reminder.

Alok lay motionless, eyes wide open. He knew that she meant what she said. He took the knife and placed it under his blanket. And he did sleep with one eye open that night, and for quite some time thereafter. He never went near Nicholas again, and if he got too close to him accidentally, Tawanda gave him an unnerving glare.

The same night Tawanda warned her brother, Manendra watched his daughter lie back in her bed. He rolled over on his side and sadly understood why his two sons kept their distance from one another. It concerned him a great deal, but not nearly as much as when Nicholas said his goodbyes three years later.

Chapter XIII

Nicholas had just finished loading Major with all his worldly possessions when Manendra stepped into the corral.

"My heart is full of sorrow," Manendra said, standing next to him. "I have known that this day would come. I have known that White Bear would search his heart and find a way to ease his mind...and then it would be time for my son to go his own separate way."

Nicholas felt sorry for Manendra. He didn't want to hurt him, yet he knew that his life would never be complete until he sought justice for what was done to his parents, even if it meant risking his life.

"What you seek is not for me to judge," he continued. "It is only my wish that you will find what it is you are looking for, and then you can come back to the land of our people. Promise me that if you ever lose your way you will search for me, and when you find me, together we will decide what is right and what is just."

Nicholas looked at him affectionately for a long moment.

"I give you my word," he swore, placing a hand on Manendra's shoulder. "You know this is something that I have to do. The depths of my soul are without spiritual rest, Father. I have slept many nights with my eyes open, waiting for this time to come. And it was you, all along, that prepared me for this journey. You have taught me many things, and for this I am grateful. Mostly, you gave me a new life, one that is strong and willing; strong enough so that I may travel alone in life without fear, and willing enough to carry my own burdens upon my back. I cannot trouble my family anymore with the things that worry my heart and are too painful for me to bear."

Nicholas held out his hand. Manendra grasped it firmly and hugged him.

"Honor the Gods, my son, so they will smile upon you...and maybe someday we *will* meet again," he said, raising his chin with pride.

"Please tell Tawanda for me," Nicholas said as he leapt on Major's back.

"Her heart will know the sadness that this brings," Manendra said with pity for his daughter. "She will know without my words."

Nicholas gave him a quick nod and headed for the trail leading into the forest. He looked back to see Manendra with his arm raised in the air. Nicholas didn't return the wave. He didn't want to make it that final. Instead, he turned Major to the trail that led into the dark woods.

He was glad to leave early, before Tawanda woke from her sleep. He missed her already and didn't know if he would ever see her again. He also didn't know that she had been awake, sitting cross-legged on her blanket and staring into the darkness. She took a knife and cut off part of her hair while a single tear rolled down her cheek. However long it would take, she would wait for him.

Major trotted lazily through the snow on the trail north. It was a cold morning and a light breeze blew powdery snow into Nicholas's face. He remembered the coon hat he made. He dug it out from his pack to keep warm. He calculated the trip would take less than half the day, if he didn't freeze to death first.

He longed to see his friend Abraham. The thought comforted him and kept his mind off the cold. It also kept him from thinking about Tawanda, his life at the village, and whether he was doing the right thing by leaving all that he knew and loved. Yet, his priorities—or more precisely, his grudges—kept him from turning back.

Around mid-day, and after thinking so much that he thought his head would burst, Nicholas saw the familiar house. Nothing had changed; the manor, blockhouses, and barn looked as they always had, with the exception of a much needed coat of paint. The King's bright colors hung from the flagpole. There was a gloomy and unnerving feeling that hung about the place, as if some great event was waiting to be unleashed.

Drawing nearer, he saw guards posted at the front doors of the house. Other guards walked the grounds in their red jackets, standing out against the snowy landscape. They didn't seem to pay him too much attention as he went straight for the barn. Apparently he didn't seem to pose any threat.

Nicholas and Major entered the barn. Inside it was dark and

eerily quiet, except for the horse letting out a large huff that echoed off the dank walls.

"Abraham?" Nicholas called out.

He paused for a reply, but none came. Major seemed a little nervous, his hooves shifting and head bobbing.

"Abraham?" he called a little louder, and a figure cautiously emerged from the shadows.

"You ain't got no business here, mountain man...or whatever it is you are," the figure said, squinting his eyes and inspecting Nicholas.

Nicholas saw that it wasn't his old friend, but a man who appeared to be in his fifties or so, with a scraggly, brownish-gray beard.

"Best if you just turn that mule around and go back to where it was you came from," he added, waiving a rusty musket in the air.

The man's clothes were filthy and stained, and the knuckles on his large hands were covered with black filth.

"I told ya ta git, mister...unless you want some lead in your chest!"

He spat on the ground and his arms tensed as he waited to see if Nicholas would make the next move.

"What are you, anyway?" he jeered. "You ain't no Injun, but ya sure do dress like one. You better start talkin', boy," he pressed, as he thrust the gun a little further in front of him.

"I'm looking for Abraham. He's a good friend of mine, and can tell you so himself if you don't believe me!"

"Ain't no Abraham here, boy! So just turn right around and..."

The man paused, wiping saliva from his beard. "Wait just a minute. Now I remember. You mean the Negro that used to work here? He's been dead a while now, ever since the old Major up an' passed on some time back."

Nicholas was devastated. He had lost one of the last friends he ever knew outside of the Mohawk.

He looked toward the window where they used to sit and talk for hours. Abraham's barrel was gone and there was no pipe waiting for him on the windowsill. But there was something.

In the corner, Nicholas saw a saddle covered with dust and some hay. He knew right away that it was the one he had given to Abe

94

the last time they were together. It was his father's saddle.

Nicholas urged Major forward a little to get close.

"Hold it right there, you," the old man snapped, raising his musket. "I ain't afraid to put a ball in ya! 'Specially in some stray that ain't worth a damn!"

"Tell me, sir," Nicholas said, "I'm not looking for any trouble and, as you can see, I'm in dire need of a saddle for my horse. Perhaps the item in the corner is of no use to you, and we may be able to settle on a price?"

The man looked a little perplexed by the offer. He steadied his musket and turned his head to see from the corner of his eye what Nicholas was referring to.

"Ain't mine to take payment fer," he said, looking back at him.

Nicholas reached into his pack for the pouch of coins that was once his father's.

"UT, UT!" blurted the man, fearful that Nicholas was about to pull a weapon on him.

Nicholas lifted the pouch to show him there was no threat.

"It's a purse of gold and silver coins," Nicholas said, rattling it as proof.

"Tol' ya, boy, ain't mine to sell," the man said, "but you can just hand that over. And don't worry, I ain't afraid of pluggin' ya one, and I mean what I say. So don't tempt me boy!"

The old man cocked his musket and smiled an evil grin of brown and black teeth.

Nicholas nodded, pretending to be outfoxed, and slowly held out the purse. Before the old man's grimy fingers could snatch it, Nicholas kicked the man's musket into his chin, discharging the weapon while Nicholas jumped down from his horse. He dashed for the corner of the barn, tossed a couple of coins on the ground, grabbed the saddle, and was back atop Major before the man even knew what hit him.

"YAH!" Nicholas yelled as Major bolted for the barn doors.

By then, some soldiers had reached the barn, weapons ready. Nicholas flew past them, knocking one to the ground, and galloped toward the main drive. He could hear the old man screaming in the distance.

"STOP HIM! HE'S A THIEF!"

A few soldiers took aim and fired. Steel balls whirred around Nicholas as Major galloped as hard and fast as he could, kicking up snow and earth. He found the road and headed north to the safety of the mountains. Nicholas pushed Major for about a mile before he let him rest. Then he got down and rubbed the horse's nose.

"Well, fella," he said with a nervous smile, "sort of like the ol' days, huh...except we weren't running from anything back then, were we?"

Nicholas placed his father's saddle on the ground and listened to see if anyone was following him.

"Don't think they'll bother us anymore today," he said, looking around. "Besides, it's paid for...under crude circumstances, mind you, but paid for." He threw the dusty saddle on Major's back, buckled it securely, and started off again. He couldn't remember a more comfortable ride, after riding bareback for almost four years.

The sun was starting to go down beyond the tips of the trees and Nicholas knew he was getting close. Many things started to look familiar to him, but it wasn't until he had come upon the far side of Garoga's east lake that he knew he was home again.

Memories of earlier days flashed before him as he rode near the shoreline. He remembered how he used to swim and fish there on many hot afternoons. He loved the lake and everything about it, but his feelings quickly changed when he found the old dirt road, now overgrown and barely visible, which led to the place he once called home.

The narrow passage was thick with weeds and young saplings. Forest vegetation claimed the edges of the once trodden road, forming a deep, snow-covered canopy that blocked most of the early evening light. He suspected the path hadn't been heavily used since that fateful day. Nicholas's stomach felt uneasy. It was hard to go any further.

He remembered the last time he stood on the road, when his head swam with terrifying sights and sounds. But now it was quiet.

The screech of a hawk jerked him back to the present. His heart raced as he pressed on.

"It's just you and me, fella," Nicholas said, urging Major forward.

He rounded the bend and came to an open field where the road ended. Mounds of charred debris poked through the snow. He could still make out where the cabin, barn, and other buildings once stood. Nothing else was recognizable, except for the open fields and distant mountains.

Nicholas got down from Major and tied him to a tree. He walked over to the remains of the cabin and sifted through the ruins. There wasn't much to be discovered except for a rusted skillet, a spoon, and some other objects of no value. He could see the remnants of the cooking stove that his mother had used so frequently, jutting out from the center of the pile. The only remains of the stone fireplace that once warmed the cabin were a few hunks of charred rock barely visible in the snow.

It was getting dark and Nicholas decided to investigate more in the morning. He collected as much firewood as possible to keep warm and prepared a crude lean-to for the evening. For some strange reason he slept well that night, almost as if he were a young child again. He had a lot of work to do the following day. It was the beginning of making things right again and finding an inner peace that he had long yearned for, to fill the hollow void in his soul.

As he drifted off to sleep, he thought of Tawanda, Manendra, and the village. He missed them and thought he would return someday when the time was right. Yet, that someday was probably far off.

Not long after Nicholas drifted into a deep slumber, a watchful eye lit a small fire in the nearby woods. He took extra precautions to make sure his presence was kept a secret. And after finishing his meal, he slept...and when the morning came, he rose much earlier than Nicholas.

Chapter XIV

The early morning air was crisp and calm as Nicholas raised his musket and seated the butt end of the stock against his shoulder. He kept the barrel sighted on the deer as it cautiously made its way toward him. The young doe occasionally lifted its twitching ears to detect any sign of a threat. When it was in range, Nicholas took a deep breath and prepared to squeeze the trigger. At the same instant, the deer bolted without warning and took off in a heartbeat.

Nicholas lowered the gun. The deer's reaction was strange, almost as if it had been spooked by something just before he pulled the trigger. He couldn't imagine what it was that had sent it on a dead run. It was very quiet and still in the woods, without so much as a leaf stirring. He assumed that the deer must have caught his scent just in the nick of time.

There was no more time left to hunt, as there were other things to get done before early afternoon. He would have to settle for the jerky in his pack, unless a rabbit found its way into the crude sling trap he had fashioned the night before.

Still a little baffled by the deer's reaction, he traced his steps back to the makeshift camp and grabbed a water flask that hung from Major's side. He gave the horse some corn for breakfast, patted him affectionately, and headed for the lake.

The top of the lake was a thin sheet of ice except for a four-foot border along the shoreline. When it was completely frozen, Nicholas thought he might try his hand at ice fishing. Nicholas lowered the flask into the water and thought fondly of ice fishing with Alok.

"Humph," he said aloud to himself. "That's odd." He hadn't any desire to think about Alok, but now, he was reminiscing about the two of them together. It even made him smile a little. Perhaps he was already homesick for his Indian family.

A muffled thump sounded behind him. The hair on the back of his neck stood up straight. He pulled his knife from his belt and spun around.

Alok's stare pierced through Nicholas's skull. His eyes were wild with fury as he had the Indian—who brandished a hatchet within inches of Nicholas's head—in a tight stranglehold around his neck. The Indian's legs buckled as he slowly sagged to the ground and rolled over. Alok held onto the blood-soaked knife as it slipped out of the savage's back.

Nicholas looked at the dead Indian in disbelief. Firmly gripping his own knife, he didn't know if he should thank Alok for saving his life...or attack him.

Alok wiped the knife on his leggings and placed it in its sheath.

"Now we are even, *my brother*," he hissed, then turned to retreat back into the woods.

In near disbelief, Nicholas watched him mount his horse and depart without another word. He lifted the dead Indian and saw that he was like the Canadian Indians that had murdered his parents. He was too young to have had any part in the slaying of his family, though, yet he was glad Alok killed him. The Indian would have certainly killed Nicholas in the same way—from behind his back, and if for no other reason other than to brag about it with his scalp.

Nicholas figured he had been trapping in the vicinity and the Indian didn't appreciate *his* land being intruded upon. He probably thought Nicholas to be an easy target, which he would have been if not for Alok. But why was Alok also there...and spying on him?

Nicholas couldn't help but feel some remorse as he gazed at the lifeless corpse. He decided to give him a proper burial, just to make things right.

Nicholas grabbed the Indian's wrists and dragged the body into a small opening about a hundred yards from the edge of the lake. He spent the rest of the morning building an open tomb five feet above the earth. He was barely able to lift the dead weight of the Indian's body and place it atop the structure. Nicholas had only part of a horse blanket, found near the charred remains of the old barn, to cover the Indian's head and upper torso with. Even one's enemy deserved some respect, he thought.

Nicholas spent the rest of the day making the lean-to a little more secure and located some tall, straight pines to construct a cabin with. He was pleased to find a snowshoe rabbit helplessly entangled in his trap—a fine meal to finish off the day.

Over dinner, next to the warm fire, thoughts of getting started on his new home made him anxious. He went over the details in his mind as it grew dark all around him. Nicholas made himself as comfortable as could. He lay facing the campfire and was soon asleep with a full belly and a loaded gun next to his side. He was careless once and wouldn't be again...even if it meant that he would have to spend every night with one eye open.

Next morning, Nicholas went right to work. He felled three trees with his hatchet in hardly any time at all, and decided a good hunt was in order. As long as he had a lean-to and fire-pit, there was no immediate urgency to start constructing his new home.

Nicholas left Major close to the shelter and headed into the forest on foot with his musket and loaded pack. It was a fine afternoon to hunt, and he was very content on doing so.

He walked for about a mile and stumbled upon a steel trap holding a fresh piece of meat. He saw that the ground had been recently disturbed...perhaps the day before. Nicholas quickly became alert, but seeing nothing out of the ordinary he reached for a dead branch on the ground.

He had never seen a metal trap before and lifted the frame with the branch for a closer look. The trap slammed shut, snapping the branch in two. Nicholas marveled at how easily the contraption sprung and how wonderful it would be to trap all sorts of game with such an odd device. He looked around to see if anyone had heard the loud clack of the steel, but he saw no one.

Nicholas quickly learned how to reset the trap. The owner wouldn't be too pleased to see its jaws empty of bait and tampered with, unless, of course, the owner was five feet above ground and stiff from cold and death. Nicholas would check on it the following day. He sort of hoped that it *was* the property of the dead Indian. The possibility of another person lurking in the woods nearby made his skin crawl.

As the day wore on, Nicholas had no luck hunting fresh venison, but he caught another hare and decided to make a meal of it that evening.

"Maybe I'll find you something different to eat tomorrow," he said to Major, "and something different for myself, huh boy? Deer meat would be a nice change."

Nicholas prepared to bed down for the evening. Feeling quite comfortable under a blanket of fur, he watched the flames of the fire lick the air. He tried to think of Tawanda, but his mind kept wandering to the day when he was a boy. A day that forever haunted him.

***

"*Nicholas?*" said a voice he hadn't heard in a long time. "*Nicholas, where are you?*"

Everything around him was black, but some things were coming into focus. Again he stood at the edge of a forest and saw dark shadows running back and forth in the distance, cloaked by thick plumes of gray and black smoke. A figure appeared from the swirling fumes and rapidly approached him. Terror froze his body. He couldn't run or scream, as the all too familiar woman in the white gown quickly advanced on him—bloodied to her waist, hatchet protruding from her skull.

"*There you are, my prince,*" said the woman. "*You didn't forget about your poor, dear mother, did you? Well, DID YOU?*"

The woman screamed then laughed, as blood spewed from her mouth and onto Nicholas.

"NOOO!" screamed Nicholas.

He ran as hard and fast as he could until he met up with an Indian thrusting a hatchet, over and over, into the bloodied body of a screaming woman. The Indian kept hacking away, and then looked up. It was Alok! Blood covered him from head to toe.

"*Now we are even, my brother!*" he devilishly grinned, while his face oddly contorted with hate. "*Even, even, even, even, even, even...*" he screamed as he thrust the hatchet up and down multiple times into the wriggling corpse.

"NOOO...STOP! PLEASE STOP!" Nicholas screamed.

***

The last word ripped through the windy night and forced him

into an upright position. He was sweating so heavily that his body shivered uncontrollably in the ice cold. The fire had burned down and he rose to fuel it. He climbed back under his blanket and pulled it tight around his chin. Staring into the fire, he remembered the last time he had that dream. It *wasn't* over. And he didn't know if it ever would be.

He woke to the same nightmare again and again throughout the night, until at last the morning light came. The best thing he could think of doing was to get right to work and cut down as many pines as he could. Now, it seemed that the cabin needed to be built as quickly as possible. He realized that there were a number of other things that needed to be done as well. And one in particular.

And so the new day began. Nicholas felled seven more pines, making ten in total, and he could halve each one to make four walls. Tomorrow he would cut more pines to frame out a roof, and then clear the rubble where the original cabin stood and salvage whatever he could find from the ruins. He was too tired to hunt or check the metal trap, and had only enough energy to give Major the last of the corn he had stashed away. His supper would have to be the last bit of jerky he kept, but he knew that he would need more food and water in the morning.

That night he was too tired to dream, and surprisingly, slept quite peaceably. He woke in the morning and wasted no time setting his snare trap and hunting for game. With hunger driving him, it wasn't long before he returned to camp with the quartered carcass of a moose that, unfortunately for the beast, crossed paths with him. And in no time, Nicholas stretched the hide while some of the meat cooked for the evening meal. For the remainder of the day he worked as hard as he could to keep his mind occupied, until it was time to bed down once again under the starlit, wintry sky.

Chapter XV

The winds had died down by the time morning came, and Nicholas decided to take advantage of the good weather to explore the wilderness. He was eager to check the trap that he had stumbled upon two days ago. Then he would get back to work on his cabin and collect more food and water for Major.

He found the trap in approximately the same area and noticed that someone had loaded it with fresh meat. Footprints in the snow seemed to approach from a southeast direction. Kneeling down to examine the trap more closely, Nicholas wondered who his new neighbor might be. Then he heard large thuds advancing toward him with great speed.

"YAAAAH!" boomed a voice.

A hard object slammed into his side, knocking him flat to the ground. A man pounced on top of Nicholas with a knife. Nicholas grabbed his wrists and wrestled his way on top. The man flung him off and had the advantage once again. Nicholas kneed him in the groin and twisted the man's wrist, making his knife drop into the snow. Then he sprang to his feet. His opponent was on his feet at the same instant and both crouched, circling each other.

His adversary wore a beaver hat and a large bear coat that cloaked most of his large frame. His face was heavily bearded, revealing only the tip of his red nose and squinting eyes.

"YAAAAH!" the man yelled again. He lowered his head and lunged at Nicholas. Both were on the ground again, rolling back and forth in the snow.

"I got ya, redskin!" the man grunted, keeping his hold on Nicholas.

"Are you sure?" strained Nicholas, rolling back on top and looking him dead in the eyes.

The woodsman relaxed his hold and looked harder at Nicholas.

"You're not a redskin!" he alleged. He swung Nicholas off him with incredible ease, pinning him to the ground. "But redskin or not, I don't take kindly to thieves! You should know better than to try and steal another man's wares!"

Nicholas threw the man off him. "I wasn't stealing anything, ya smelly varmint!" he yelled, holding him down with his forearm. "Just never saw one before!"

The man looked at him and a smile formed on his lips.

"What?" he said. "Just never saw one?" He broke into a deep laugh that was broken by fits of coughing.

"Don't see what's so funny about it," Nicholas said with disgust, which made the man laugh even harder.

"Don't see what's so funny?" he roared. "Funniest thing I ever heard! Now, get off me greenhorn!" he bellowed, and with another great burst of strength threw Nicholas to the side. Nicholas jumped back to his feet. The man sat on the ground, brushing away snow from his sleeves, and trying to contain himself.

"Well," the man said, "you're either a terrible thief…or you're an idiot!" He looked up with a grin. "I'm going with the latter, my friend, unless you can persuade me otherwise." He stuck out his hand.

Nicholas just looked at him.

"So, you gonna help me up?" he said, still grinning.

Nicholas cautiously walked over and extended his hand. The man grabbed his hand, pulled Nicholas to the ground then got to his feet. He brushed off a little more snow and put his hands on his knees, looking down at Nicholas.

"Yup!" he said with a smirk. "I was right. Idiot!"

Nicholas rose to his feet and countered, "Apparently, sir, you are the idiot…or not a very good trapper. If I wanted to steal your trap, I would have done so two days ago. But seeing the contraption empty with no game all that time, I figured it mustn't be of much value."

The grizzly man stood up straight and, with a nod of approval, said, "Fair enough. I'd like to know the name of the man who can equal his opponent with words, unless of course, you aren't called by anything."

"I have a name," Nicholas said, wiping his mouth with his sleeve. "It's Nicholas Dunne."

The man threw back his chest and yelled excitedly, "Well, I'll be! Nicholas Dunne!" and hooted some more.

"It would please me to know the name of the man who laughs at everything, even when trying to cut my throat," Nicholas replied, brushing snow from his arms and waist.

The woodsman walked toward him with his arms open. Nicholas jumped back and crouched into a wrestling stance.

"It's me!" the man cried. "Andrew! Andrew Smith!"

Nicholas couldn't quite remember where or when he had heard the name.

"Aaaw," the man said, flinging his arms in the air. "Johnson Hall, remember? About four years ago we raced against each other on foot?"

A big smile spread across Nicholas's face. "Andrew Smith? Andrew Smith!" he hollered with delight.

"Before your very eyes!" Andrew said, holding his arms open.

"HA, HA!" Nicholas yelled, and embraced Andrew with a giant bear hug. "How the hell are ya, Andrew Smith?"

"Couldn't be finer, if there was such a thing!" he winked.

They danced in the snow, holding onto one another.

"Let me take a better look at ya!" said Andrew, holding Nicholas's shoulders and stepping back a bit. "I heard that you'd gone to live with the Turtles around Canajoharie way, and by the looks of it, you did just that. Tell me, how is Manendra these days?"

Nicholas looked puzzled. "You know Manendra?"

"Any man who ever wandered all the parts of this countryside knows Manendra. We *are* talkin' about the chief's only son, aren't we?"

"Chief's son? I didn't know he was the son of a chief!"

Andrew scratched his beard. "Didn't know, you say? Suppose it's possible that they could keep it a secret from ya. Might make some sense too," he said looking up before looking back at him. "Manendra has a blood son...Alok, I believe...stubborn fella...a little hot-headed?" he said as he made a crazy-headed gesture with his hands.

"Yes!" exclaimed Nicholas, still confused.

"Well, it's only natural that they would want to keep it a secret from you. After all, it's only a matter of time before the tribal women will elect Manendra as the next chief. And that means Alok would be next in line, wouldn't it?"

Everything made sense now—the jealousy, the avoidance, the foiled attempt to get rid of him. Alok was protecting his rite of passage and saw Nicholas as a threat. And all of it could have been avoided if he had known—or was told—so he could reassure Alok that he wasn't, nor ever would be, interested in becoming a chief! Then again, it probably wouldn't have mattered. Alok wouldn't have believed him anyway.

"Well, enough about that," said Andrew, now sitting on a log. "What brings you back to these parts?"

Nicholas told him how he could never get over the loss of his parents and vowed to seek vengeance. He told Andrew that he believed the killers were outcasts from an eastern Algonquin tribe and forced to the north, but he wasn't too sure. He had returned to Garoga as a means to begin his search, to the place where he last saw his parent's murderers, and hoped he would meet up with them again. He assured Andrew that if he ever did get a hold of them, they would be sorry for what they did.

Nicholas also told him about how he had cut down trees to make a cabin for himself and reclaim the land that was rightly his, but prior to that, he spoke of how Alok had saved him from being cut to pieces by a Canadian Indian at the lake. He also said to him that it was repayment for saving Alok's life years ago.

Andrew listened intently, absorbing everything that Nicholas told him. When Nicholas finished, Andrew guaranteed him that, he too, wouldn't be able to sleep if his parents were murdered with intent, and agreed that getting revenge was the just thing to do.

After they had visited for a while, Andrew stood and said, "My friend, soon it will be dark, and I can't think of a better way to continue this reunion than over a hot meal and a hard drink. Tell you what…gather up your things, load up your horse, and follow my path about a couple miles south. I have some traps to check and will meet you back at my place." Andrew pulled a pack from behind a tree. "You can't miss it with a good nose. How does chicken and biscuits smothered in gravy sound?"

Nicholas couldn't remember the last time he had chicken. And a cozy place to bed down for the night would greatly satisfy his stiff, tired joints.

"Sounds like heaven, right now!" he said.

"Then, so it is," Andrew said. "There's a barn for your horse with plenty to eat. Make sure you fatten him up. Tomorrow we'll take a look at your camp and maybe that Indian of yours. If my hunch is right, he's the one that's been tampering with my traps."

Nicholas quickly went back for his things. He couldn't wait to see Andrew's place, but mostly he wanted to get Major out of the cold and give him food. Filling his own stomach with a good, hot meal was going to be a treat, and he wondered what Andrew's woman would be like. Certainly a meal that fine had to be prepared by a woman's hands, and hopefully she wouldn't mind an unexpected visitor.

Chapter XVI

Finding Andrew's dwelling was as easy as he said. Even without a path to follow, he could smell the roasting fowl. Nicholas was surprised by how large the cabin was. The outer walls couldn't have been more than seven feet high, but it was at least forty feet long and twenty feet wide. The roof was framed and shingled with spruce, and a large stone chimney clung to the side, bellowing gray-blue smoke into the darkening sky.

The barn was slightly smaller, just big enough to house a few large animals. There was a storage shed and chicken coop nearby. Nicholas thought that it must have taken some time to plan and construct the perfect placement for each building.

He led Major to the barn and saw an open stall full of hay and oats situated next to a squealing pig. There was a wagon at the far end loaded with barrels, which he assumed to be gunpowder. Nicholas thought that it could be very comfortable for either man or beast, especially when one had spent the past few nights in a cold lean-to.

He took the saddle and blanket from Major's back, and the horse looked at him almost as if he was enjoying the comfort of the place as well. Major immediately shuffled over to the food, gave it a quick snuff or two, and dug right in.

The barn door flung open and Andrew led his horse inside.

"See you found the place," he said. He lit an oil lamp that hung from a support beam.

"I can't thank you enough for the invitation! Nice place you've made for yourself and the wife."

Andrew laughed. "I'll agree that it does suit my needs, but she's not the one that does the cookin' since, I ain't married or attached!"

"Oh," said Nicholas, a little surprised. "I just assumed you had a woman present when you said there was dinner waiting. No hard feelings, I hope?"

"None at all, my friend," Andrew said, putting an arm around

Nicholas's shoulder. "I think the animals are well provided for. What do you say about gettin' ourselves inside? Hungry?"

"Sure am! Lead the way," said Nicholas.

The cabin was warm and cheerful. There were no separate rooms. The vast open space was furnished with a table and two chairs, an old cupboard, a cot in one of the corners for Andrew, and another as a spare. There was a bear rug near the fireplace and the walls were decorated with traps, snowshoes, and other tools of the trade. A small painting of a landscape hung in crooked fashion on one wall. But what aroused Nicholas's attention the most, was the wonderful smell of the cooking food. Nicholas's belly growled with hunger.

"Please, make yourself comfortable while I heat these biscuits," Andrew said, retrieving a cast iron pot from the mantle and placing it next to the fire.

Nicholas hung his blanket and leather shirt near the doorway and sat in one of the chairs. Andrew opened the cupboard and took out two mugs and a large jug.

"I always like some spirits before *and* after my meal," he said cheerfully. "Helps the digestion." He poured the dark brown liquid into Nicholas's glass.

Nicholas took one smell of the concoction and winced. Andrew laughed a hearty one.

"I apologize, Nick ol' boy. I should have known that you were probably unacquainted with the taste of liquor."

"My father would keep some at home, to entertain with, but my lips never touched the stuff," said Nicholas. "I wasn't allowed to get within arm's reach of it. And most Mohawk believe it to be the spit of the Devil, so to speak. But my father believed that as long as it didn't play on your senses, he didn't think that God would mind if a man had a taste here or there."

"I concur...and I can't see a more fitting moment to partake of the good Lord's greatest gift, although some colonists—mostly the women folk—would agree with the Indians. But no mind." With that, Andrew raised his tin cup to make a toast. Nicholas followed suit.

"To friends," he said with the tip of his head. *"Whether alive or dead, 'tis all the same...with this cup, we're all fair game."* Andrew slugged it down in one big gulp and slammed the cup on the table.

"Whew!" he exhaled.

Nicholas held his glass out, tipped his head back, and emptied the contents into his throat. The liquid burned, and he felt as though his lungs would explode. He keeled over and coughed. Andrew laughed as hard as he ever had in a long time. Nicholas wasn't as amused, as he tried to speak and breathe at the same time.

"Definitely the work of the Devil," he said hoarsely, barely audible. "I can see why Mother kept me away from such vile stuff. It surely would have sent me to my grave at a young age!"

Andrew thought he would die from laughing. And just when he thought he couldn't laugh any harder, Nicholas stuck out the glass and said with a hiccup, "I should like more, if you please." Andrew almost fell from his chair.

After a few more rounds followed by a good meal, Nicholas and Andrew pulled their chairs next to the fire. Andrew told him that his parents were doing well on a farm near the town of New Amsterdam, which was populated primarily of Dutch immigrants who settled on the nearby river. He had left his parent's farm about a year ago when he was sixteen, to explore the wilderness and become a full-time trapper. He farmed a small piece of land to produce winter staples, mainly for the animals, but for the most part lived by trading and selling pelts. He had just finished construction of the hen house and storage shed that month and in good timing, for it was the perfect season for trapping muskrat, fisher, and beaver.

"There's an abundance of fowl and beast to sustain quite a comfortable life," Andrew said as he puffed on a pipe.

The tobacco aroma reminded Nicholas of his talks with Abraham. How he missed those days. Andrew noticed Nicholas's enjoyment and offered him a second pipe, which was politely refused. Sometimes it was better not to remember the things that meant the most, and somehow he didn't think that filling one's lungs with pungent smoke could be healthy for the body, even though he witnessed a lot of pipe smoking in the Indian village.

"Will be nice to have a neighbor, especially in these times of strife," Andrew said, tapping the pipe bowl in his palm and throwing the remnants into the fireplace. "Safety in numbers is what they say."

"Times of strife?" repeated Nicholas. "Meaning..."

Andrew was about to re-light his pipe, but looked at Nicholas as if he had two heads.

"My God, you don't know, do you?"

Nicholas scrunched his brow.

"Nicholas," Andrew said in a serious tone, "we're at war with the Brits!"

Nicholas couldn't believe what he had just heard and asked Andrew to repeat himself. He was shocked and mortified. How could he have not known? Then again, after Andrew explained the most recent events in Boston and throughout the rest of the country, he figured that it really didn't concern the Indians. It sounded more like the colonists wanting to break free from the Crown. He couldn't have known that eventually the Mohawk would join with England to try and save their land from pioneer expansion.

"My father and brothers are thinking of joining the Cause," Andrew said solemnly.

"And you?" said Nicholas.

"I don't see the purpose of men killing men. For what? Taxation...or land disputes? If its land they want, there's a whole frontier out west to be explored and had. I ask you...what price should a man pay for his life and for the lives of his family?"

"You can't put a price on freedom, if that's the case," said Nicholas. "Then again, I wholeheartedly agree with you that it isn't right to spill a man's blood only for the purpose of gaining land, power, or riches. But if it's for my livelihood, then I might have to think a little harder on what would be the right thing to do."

"Well said, my friend," agreed Andrew. "Let's just hope it doesn't come to that for the likes of us! Another sip or two before we bed down for the night?"

"I should say so," stammered Nicholas, now feeling the full effects of the liquor all at once. "And might I add, that your hosbitality is by far the most hosbidable of all hosbidaliblies."

Andrew laughed a bellyful as he poured them a drink and chimed in cheerfully to say, "The words of a true gentlemen...drunken words...but true. God save the King, me lord," he said, mocking the British as they touched mugs and filled themselves with more spirits.

They drank throughout a good part of the night. Nicholas had

111

instantly felt right at home the moment he stepped into the cabin. He could picture his new home being as comfortable and manageable as Andrew's was. There was only one thing missing, though. Tawanda. If only there was some way he could see her again. It had only been a few days, but he already missed her terribly.

For the past four years, she had been constantly near him and it made him feel good inside. Yet, he knew that there was much work to be done before he could even think about making a trip back to the village, and he was eager to get started right away.

The drink put his mind at ease and he slept well throughout the rest of the night. There were no dreams or nightmares, and Nicholas thought he could get used to having a sip or two each evening.

When morning came, Nicholas's brain felt like it would pound through his skull. Still, after breakfast, he was full of exuberance to show Andrew his new home.

Chapter XVII

Nicholas and Andrew parted ways in the morning, with the agreement to meet up later in the day at Nicholas's camp. Nicholas thought he could cut down a couple of trees before Andrew arrived from checking his traps. He admired Andrew's courage in setting out on his own and making a comfortable existence in the sometimes formidable wild.

Just as he was about to trim the branches from a freshly felled tree, a shot rang out in the distance. Nicholas waited for a time and decided to get back to work. He assumed it was Andrew and wasn't too concerned.

"*Hellooo!*" a voice called from the trees shortly thereafter.

Nicholas lowered his hatchet and could just make out a figure walking his horse toward the camp.

"This way!" yelled Nicholas, flailing an arm as Andrew entered from the east side of the woods.

"Got something for ya!" said Andrew as he approached. He slid a large, dark animal from his horse's back onto the ground. Nicholas walked over and saw it was a neatly gutted black bear that must have originally weighed around three hundred pounds.

"I figured you could use a nice rug for your new home," Andrew said, then studied the landscape and surrounding grounds.

"Next to the fireplace!" said Nicholas. "Which I recollect will be somewhere in that area." He pointed in the direction of a small clearing.

"And with any luck, we should have a fine cabin for ya in about one month's time, if we get right to it," Andrew said, pulling a large axe from his pack.

"We?" said Nicholas, surprised by the gesture. "That's very kind of you, Andrew, but I can't ask for any favors. You've already shown me great kindness already, and besides..."

"Don't hand me any of that babbling," he interrupted. "I said it was going to be nice to have a neighbor around, and that's what neighbors are for. Not to mention the fact that you're staying with me until the cabin is built, then you're on your own. You're gonna need better shelter than that by the time spring comes," he said, pointing at the crude lean-to. "You'll need to get plenty of things done if you want good crops to harvest."

Nicholas looked at him and smiled. "I won't know how to repay you."

"You'll think of a way, I'm sure," Andrew said with a chuckle. "For now, you get that bear stretched, and I'll see to pickin' out the trees we need to log."

The thought of living in the lean-to for another two or three months didn't appeal to Nicholas at all. With Andrew's help, he could have a cabin built quickly, and in the meantime, he wouldn't have to worry so much about food and a warm place for Major. And Andrew's company would be most welcome.

Nicholas told Andrew that together they would tend to the traps and winter chores around his place, and he wouldn't take no for an answer. Andrew agreed without any resistance and the pact was made with a single handshake.

They worked with hardly any rest throughout the passing weeks and soon had the four walls of the cabin erected. They immediately began on the roof. The weekends seemed like a vacation from the hard work. Most of their time was spent trapping, tending to the animals, or cleaning the barn. They had quite a few pelts stored from their labors, and one day Andrew announced that they would take a day off and make a trip to John's Town—re-named Fort Johnstown due to the war—where the nearest trading post was located.

Nicholas couldn't wait to make the trip. He was ready to see the town again and eager to mingle with the colonists and catch up on any news about the war that lingered throughout the land.

A week later they set out for the trading post and arrived in town to see swarms of people gathered in the square. A British officer read from a scroll, informing the colonists that disloyalty to the Crown would be deemed treason, punishable by imprisonment and/or death. Nicholas and Andrew joined the crowd to listen in. It was obvious that some colonists would remain loyal to the King, probably out of fear for their own necks, while others clearly didn't favor the idea at all.

Some colonists voiced their opinions, concerned about protecting their families and land.

"All those who remain loyal to His Majesty will be granted the right to live of their own free will," the officer announced. "Those of you who choose to do otherwise, and proclaim defiance, will be sought out, tried, and convicted. If you so dare as to commit crimes against this proclamation, then you are considered to be the enemy and, in doing so, your families will be outcasts and your homes burned. All property that is left will be reclaimed by His Majesty."

There was a lot of rumbling in the crowd and people started to turn on each other.

Andrew pulled Nicholas aside. "He talks of free will," he said, speaking quietly and looking uneasily over his shoulder, "but I'm beginning to suspect that we're in the midst of a dictatorship...and not a democracy. Maybe our freedom is at stake! These are not choices for the good of the people, but in fact seem more like threats with dire consequences."

He took Nicholas's arm and casually whispered in his ear, "I'll go to the trading post alone, and with any luck, will gather more news of this unrest. I advise you to do the same at the tavern across the street."

"Agreed." said Nicholas. "I, too, would like to know more of this war."

"I'll meet you at the tavern...but be careful! Don't engage in any conversation with anyone! Get yourself a drink," he said, handing Nicholas some money. "and listen to what they're saying with both ears. I fear there may be spies on both sides lurking about!"

Andrew patted his arm to wish him luck and led his horse toward the other side of town.

Nicholas tied Major in front of the tavern and entered the shadowy interior. There were many men inside engaged in heated conversation over what should or shouldn't be done about their situation. On the advice of Andrew, Nicholas did as he was told. He headed right to the bar and ordered a drink.

One man stood on a table, bellowing passionately and thrusting a mug in the air.

"I'll not be bullied by John Johnson and his band of rogues," he balked. "I have worked hard for my land, which gives me the right to do with my property as I wish, not be told to bow down to a King thousands of miles away, and who considers the likes of us to be misfits."

"Hear, hear!" encouraged some of the patrons. Nicholas sipped his drink, pretending to be uninterested.

"Furthermore, should we stand in allegiance with those that have penalized us with harsh taxes, and who see to it that our prosperity is constantly harassed?"

The tavern's door flung open.

"Out of the way!" yelled a British officer, as he and five other armed soldiers shoved their way toward the man. "Out of the way, all of you!"

"There is your protection!" the man yelled, as the troops approached him. "It's all lies!" he screamed, as the soldiers pulled him from the table and dragged him toward the door. "This is not free will! Lies, I tell you! Lies!" The soldiers dragged him by his heels from the tavern and into a nearby courtyard just off the street.

Everyone exited the tavern and swarms of people gathered about the side streets to watch the spectacle. The man was screaming, kicking his legs, and yelling profanities at the soldiers. They propped him in a kneeling position, secured his wrists around his back, and tied a cloth in his mouth to stifle his voice. An officer entered the center square on horseback, quickly dismounted, pulled a pistol from his waist, and shot him in the back of the head.

The man slumped lifelessly to the ground headfirst, and a great stillness swept over the stunned audience.

"This man," yelled the officer to the crowd, "could have saved himself if he only heeded to the instructions clearly given to every one of you! And I'll say to you again—those of you, MAN, WOMAN, OR CHILD, that defy the wishes of His Majesty, will not know any mercy. THIS, INSTEAD," he bellowed, pointing his pistol to the unfortunate man, "WILL BE YOUR FATE!"

A woman in the crowd screamed and rushed to the man, whom lay in a pool of streaming blood.

"MURDERERS!" she screamed, as she knelt on the ground and cradled the victim in her arms. "Mark this day, for *GOD* will see to it that every one of you are thrust into the bowels of the Devil's lair for taking the life of an innocent man!"

"Remove her!" ordered the officer, and a few of his men immediately dragged her from the body.

"I hope you are all struck down by the might of the Lord's hand," she cried as they carried her off, "and I will laugh, knowing that you will all ROT IN HELL!"

The officer got back on his horse, and while trying to hold the animal steady he barked out, "I order all of you to depart for your homes and families. Think about what you witnessed here today, and decide where your loyalty lies!" The officer left without haste, leaving the crowd to deal with their grief and terror.

Nicholas watched as the people disbanded and the soldiers carried off the dead man. *My God, this is murder!* he thought to himself.

Andrew appeared from the crowd with his horse and again grabbed Nicholas's arm. "We have to leave! Now!" he whispered. "An army of redcoats are only a few miles from the town and it's safer for us to go back home."

Nicholas agreed, and they mounted their horses and went the longer way around town to head back north. They decided to retreat to Andrew's place for the rest of the day and discuss the events over dinner.

"I saw what they did to that poor fellow," said Andrew as he lit his pipe. "Maybe my father and brothers are right in joining the Cause."

"I don't know what to make of it, except for the fact that what I saw was indeed unjust," said Nicholas. "Yet, I'm still wary about it all. I thought my feelings were stirred enough to join this march to independence, but I also haven't fulfilled my own personal obligations."

"Nick," said Andrew, leaning forward over the table and looking his friend square in the eyes, "I'm going to join my father and brothers."

Nicholas sat back in his chair and lowered his head. "I thought you might," he said with some disappointment.

"I have no animosities to keep me here, such as yourself, and I

117

understand why you can't…and won't…involve yourself for the time being. As for me, I cannot wait for trouble to come, and I feel that it's the just thing to do. I have to go where my family is…to look out for them!"

"When?" said Nicholas.

"In a few weeks," he said. "That's when I suspect your cabin will be completely done. Then I'll head for Albany or Saratoga. Men have been gathering there in anticipation of a much greater conflict to come."

Nicholas, seeing that Andrew was serious about seeing to his family's safety, wanted to tell him to leave immediately, but he knew that Andrew wouldn't go until his friend was settled, as Nicholas would have done the same for him.

"I'll keep an eye on your home so that it's not disturbed while you're away," Nicholas promised. "I'm sure that the whole matter of war will be done away with soon, and we'll be having another drink together in the near future."

"I would hate to think any other," said Andrew. "And on that, my friend, if you don't object, I think I'll retire for the rest of the night."

"Please do, ole boy. And if you don't object, I think that I may watch the fire for a bit and have a little more whiskey, after such an unfortunate day."

"Be my guest," Andrew said, as he climbed in his bed and wrapped himself in his covers. "With all hope, tomorrow will be brighter. Good night, friend. Sleep sound."

"Night, lad," Nicholas said quietly, and he sipped whiskey and stared into the fire while reviewing the day's events. When his muscles ached and his head began to swim, he finally retreated to his bed. He was plagued by nightmares the rest of the night, but none that woke him. They seemed less powerful and not as clear, which suited him fine.

In the weeks ahead, they agreed to spend less time on trapping and more time on the cabin. As soon as the roof and fireplace were complete, a small enclosure was attached to the house for Major. Nicholas filled it with hay and food from Andrew's storage shed, and thought it would suffice until he could erect a new barn.

After the work was complete, Nicholas and Andrew had their final meal together and talked for quite a few hours. In the morning Nicholas awoke, dressed, and stepped out into the cool air. His friend was long gone without so much as a goodbye and Nicholas was glad in a way, since sending off Andrew would have made for a sad beginning to the day. There seemed to be enough sadness in his life without sending out an invitation for more. Besides, there was plenty of work to get done. Especially now that Andrew wasn't there to help out.

Nicholas buttoned up Andrew's cabin and headed north for his own home. He knew that he had to keep his mind occupied, since the days, weeks, and months ahead without his friend would be lonely. He hoped it would be sooner than later before he saw him again. And he didn't know how long that would be.

Chapter XVIII

Over the next few months, Nicholas managed to construct a small barn and other outer buildings, and in the spring he began preparing the field to plant crops. He thought of Tawanda every day and almost had the notion to visit the village to see her again. But the work kept him busy and he never seemed to find the time. If he saw her again it would be extremely difficult to leave, so he abandoned the idea. He always kept her in the back of his mind though, and felt that they would somehow be together again. Yet, the days without her turned into months, and the months into years.

He kept his word to Andrew and watched over his place. He heard nothing from him during the four years since he had left, and he didn't know if Andrew was dead or alive. But he made sure that his friend's home would be ready upon his return.

Every once in a while Nicholas would venture to Fort Johnstown to trade pelts, stock up on provisions, and visit the tavern to get news of the war. It had crossed his mind to join the Americans in the fight against the British, but since Washington's army had finally cornered the British General Cornwallis, he quickly abandoned the notion. He couldn't afford to get hurt or killed before he resolved his past. And while the years went by, he more or less kept to himself.

One day, while visiting the fort, he lumbered into the tavern for a quick drink. It was quiet inside. Fewer people gathered in public since the poor colonist was murdered years earlier, and the town was still governed by the British.

He noticed two men talking in low tones to one another. He could barely make out what they were saying, but something they said caught his attention. He took his drink and cautiously approached the men, who were sitting at a table in a dark corner.

"Pardon, gents," he said, "may I sit with you for some company?"

The men looked at him as if they weren't too happy with his bold proposal.

After a few long seconds, Nicholas—feeling a little uneasy—tipped his head apologetically and said, "Forgive me for the intrusion. I'll leave you to yourselves," and walked back toward the bar.

Halfway across the room one of the men spoke up. "You look familiar, mister. What's your name?"

Nicholas guessed that it *was* possible to be recognized, though most people wouldn't have known him from his earlier years. He grew his beard and hair long and thick, for warmth during the cold winters and as a barrier against the spring and summer pests that swarmed in droves throughout the northern woods.

Nicholas turned and went back to the table, and in a low voice replied, "The name is Nicholas Dunne. I live in the area of Garoga."

The men looked at each other, and one of them kicked a chair out from under the table as a gesture for him to sit.

"Thank you," said Nicholas. "Forgive me for asking, but I couldn't help overhearing that there was trouble in the township of New Amsterdam. May I inquire as to what you were speaking of?"

One of the men leaned forward to rest his arms on the table, holding his drink with both hands.

"It was said that a farmer was attacked by some renegade Indians. An eyewitness said they were Canadian redskins and not the Mohawk that were harassing some settlers in that area just recently."

"Do you have the name of the poor soul?" asked Nicholas, dreading what the answer might be.

The man looked at his partner. "Smith, I reckon...Henry Smith. Sound right, John?"

The other man nodded, took a big gulp of beer, and said, "Believe so...'tis what they say."

Nicholas shook his head.

The first man asked Nicholas, "Did you know him?"

"I knew *of* him," Nicholas said and took a sip of whiskey. "Tell me," he said leaning back in his chair, "were there women and children present?"

"There was a woman, probably the wife, but supposedly she'd gotten away. Fled to a neighbor's house, is how the story goes. There are three sons, but all three are away fighting the war. Why do you ask?"

121

"No reason," replied Nicholas. "Just hate to hear if there are young ones involved." He hoped that they bought his answer. He didn't want to get into details about Andrew and his family for fear that the men were British spies. Instead, Nicholas rose from his seat and placed a silver coin on the table.

"Well, I've taken up enough of your time and do appreciate the company. Don't get much these days in the mountains. I insist that you have a drink on my behalf. It'll be dark soon and I must get back home."

The men silently nodded and eyed him curiously before snatching up the coin.

Nicholas left the tavern thinking about Andrew. He hoped that his friend was okay. The war had gone on longer than anyone could have imagined and, according to various reports, many men were killed, wounded, or missing. He had a dreadful feeling that he might never see Andrew again. He couldn't bear the thought of Andrew's home being vacant and dark, with no lights burning and no one there to visit. It had seemed that whenever Nicholas found any kind of good fortune, whether through love or friendship, something was always there to take it away. It was the only thing in his life that he was getting used to.

He decided to take the trail to Andrew's cabin to make sure that it hadn't been vandalized. Some men in the tavern had warned him to be on the lookout for Canadian Indians, who were last seen around the hamlet of Broadalbin heading northwest, which would eventually put them in the vicinity of the lakes of Garoga. Nicholas wondered if these were the same band of Indians he was looking for. He knew that the odds were great, but the best person to identify those who killed his mother and father, was Manendra.

Nicholas knew that he couldn't see Manendra as long as the war raged on. He had heard a while back that the Mohawk had sided with the British, mainly because of their ties to Major Johnson. The Major kept peace with the Iroquois by trying to convince the English throne that it would be wise to let the native Indians hold onto their lands, and in return, the Iroquois could be a very useful ally, especially if their French neighbors to the north attempted any new assaults. The Indians, argued Johnson, could be used as scouts and warriors against the Algonquin Indians who would side with the French. And now that the war raged on, the Iroquois—mainly the Mohawk—thought it would be wiser to fight the Americans in order to hold on to what was promised them. They were tired of being pushed out of the lands they had controlled long before the first white man ever set foot in the New World. Even though Nicholas chose not to participate in the war, both sides could still hate him, and that was primarily why he kept his distance from most people, which unfortunately, meant Tawanda as well.

Nicholas was only a fraction of a mile from Andrew's cabin when he caught a whiff of smoke in the air. Immediately his senses were at full alert, and he stopped Major to get a better direction of where the smell might be coming from. He knew that it couldn't be the fire from his cabin, since the odor was too strong, and his place was about two miles away. Better still, it wasn't strong enough to think that it was a building or any part of the forest ablaze. Either there was a campfire close by in the woods, or someone had made himself at home in Andrew's cabin.

Nicholas urged his horse forward until he saw the faint yellow glow of a window through the early darkness. He got down from Major and tied him to a tree. He pulled his musket from the saddle and crept closer to the cabin until he was up against the front side of it. As quietly and vigilantly as possible, he peeked in the window and saw the silhouette of a figure sitting in front of the fire, his back to the door. There were no sounds coming from the interior except for the occasional pop and crackle of a burning log. Nicholas didn't think there was anyone else in the cabin, and figured that it was probably a stray taking advantage of the opportunity to warm himself in the vacant dwelling.

Nicholas stood next to the door. It was slightly ajar, with just a crack of light escaping through the opening. He carefully pushed it open and it creaked alarmingly on its rusty hinges. He was sure the intruder would leap from his chair at the sound, but he didn't move a muscle. Nicholas thought he was either deaf, drunk...or both.

He opened the squeaky door just enough to squeeze through. With the barrel of the musket extended in front of him, he slowly approached the stranger until the gun was two inches from the back of his head.

"If you make a single move, sir, I promise that it will be your last," warned Nicholas. Still, the man didn't move one bit.

"For your sake, there should be a very good reason why you took it upon yourself to occupy this house uninvited," he continued, quite nervously. "Before I kill you, I'll have your name sir, so I may know what to mark above your grave?"

But there was no response. Nicholas became agitated. He placed the tip of the barrel next to the man's temple and cocked the hammer.

"My patience is wearing thin," Nicholas hissed. "I asked you to identify yourself and this will be the last time the request passes beyond my lips. I'll not ask again! You have but one more chance to save yourself." A bead of sweat ran down Nicholas's temple. "What is your name?"

"Hello, Nicholas."

Nicholas froze. He slowly lowered the musket to get a better look at the man. Then he found his voice.

"Andrew?" said Nicholas. "Is it really you?"

The man nodded.

Nicholas placed the musket on the floor and knelt down beside him, putting a hand on his arm. Andrew looked as if he had aged twenty years. He was wrapped in a blanket, staring with distant eyes into the fire. An empty whiskey jug was overturned at his muddy feet. But Nicholas could tell that he was more than just drunk. Nicholas saw pain and emptiness in his eyes.

"Andrew, my friend, I never thought I would see you again!" Nicholas said with relief. "When did you get back? Today? Yesterday? I thought you might have been killed, since there was no word from you for four years!"

Andrew looked toward Nicholas but not at him, then gazed back into the fire.

"All is lost, my good friend," Andrew whispered in a tone full of defeat and despair. "I am lost."

"You are not lost, but are here…in the safety of your home!" Nicholas enlightened, trying to comfort him. "Andrew, you must get up and into bed! Can you do that for me?"

Andrew nodded, and Nicholas slid his arms around his friend's upper body and raised him to his feet. Andrew was mostly dead weight as Nicholas dragged him to his cot and lay him down as gently as he could.

"LOOK ALIVE MEN!" Andrew bellowed, which took Nicholas by surprise. "BE SHARP, and aim at the center of the coat! The white…the straps…crossed," he mumbled before snoring heavily in his bed.

Nicholas covered him with a blanket and took off his boots. Andrews's socks were bloody and crusted to his skin. He gently took them off as Andrew slept, and saw that his feet were horribly blistered. He left the cabin and put Major in the barn. He grabbed some water and whiskey from his pack and noticed that there was no horse in the stable where Andrew usually kept it corralled. Now he knew why his friend's feet were blistered. He had walked a great distance to get home.

He re-entered the cabin, found some clean cloth, and washed and sterilized Andrew's feet with some liquor to help ward off infection. He bandaged them, covered them with the blanket, and then went across the room to lie down on his own bed.

Throughout the night, he woke to Andrew screaming or crying out incoherent words. Nicholas knew it were the nightmares. Something that he was all too familiar with.

Chapter XIX

Andrew woke to heavenly aromas filling the cabin. He wasn't sure where he was, but after looking around a bit he recognized the familiar interior of his home. Nicholas was huddled near the fireplace, cooking eggs and bacon next to a pot of steaming coffee.

Nicholas heard him stir. "Morning, Andrew," he said, trying to be as cheerful as possible. "Hope you're hungry!" He placed the meal on the table.

Andrew held his head and tried to leave his bed, but moaned with pain and fell back into his cot the moment his swollen feet touched the hard floor.

"Hold on," Nicholas said, as he rushed over to help him stand.

"Thank you Nick," Andrew murmured, slowly limping to his chair.

Nicholas placed some breakfast in front of him, but Andrew just stared at it.

"Try putting something in your belly," said Nicholas. "Unless, of course, you find my cookin' to be undesirable," he added, trying to make light of the situation.

Andrew picked up a fork and forced some food into his mouth. They ate in silence. Nicholas thought it would be better to engage in conversation when Andrew was ready.

After breakfast Andrew sipped coffee, holding his cup close to his lips with both hands.

"My father was killed," Andrew said with no emotion, looking into space. "I looked all over for my mother, but couldn't find her...so I don't know what has become of her. I can only guess."

"Your brothers?" said Nicholas.

"Dead," he replied, barely audible. "It was this damn war that got 'em," he said with much hate in his voice.

"Andrew, what happened after you left? I mean, of course, if you're willing to discuss the matter," Nicholas said.

After a brief pause, Andrew took another sip of coffee and

shook his head, as if trying to collect his thoughts.

"I enlisted at Albany...me and about fifteen other men," he began. "I sold my horse for personal supplies and our detachment was sent to Ticonderoga...to guard a fort there from the possibility of an attack of advancing British under the command of General Burgoyne."

Nicholas listened intently and let him go on without uttering a single word.

"On July the fourth, we had gotten news that there was a force of eight thousand men advancing quickly toward the fort. Since we were only three thousand strong, it was decided that we would abandon the fort and travel along the Hubbardton Road. The British followed us, and around the sixth of the month they caught up with our forces to the rear. Some were killed, but for the most part, the strength of our army was able to retreat to the safety of Fort Edward, south of Lake George."

Andrew kept staring, as if the events were unfolding once again in front of his eyes. He slid his cup across the table for Nicholas to fill with more coffee, and rubbed his neck and head hard.

"From there, we left for Saratoga," he continued. "It was speculated that Burgoyne was marching south with all intentions to fight. And that's what we did...fight...twice at Saratoga. The first in the field of a local man named Freeman." Andrew laughed a little. "Hell, that was a coincidence," he mused, more or less to himself.

"It was the first time that I had ever really seen any action. You know in your head that some men might die, but before the initial fighting broke out we were somewhat hypnotized by the sights and sounds of the battlefield...almost as if it were unreal in a way."

Andrew thought for a moment, reliving it in his mind.

"There we stood," he said, "in lines only a hundred yards or so away from the enemy. The ground between the two forces exploded from cannon shot, but at first, nothing came close enough to hurt anyone. Despite the danger, I felt at peace with myself," Andrew said, with a strange, yet content look on his face.

"I remember that it was a beautiful September day. Cows grazed nearby as if there wasn't a care in the world. Flags on both sides waved high in the air and the music...the music was everywhere. How odd it was to hear drums and fifes playing cheerful notes. That is, until the first shots were fired."

Andrew's face turned solemn, again staring into nowhere. Nicholas found himself picturing the events as Andrew's experience unfolded with his words.

"The enemy fired the first volley into our center it seemed, and the men that formed our front line fell silently to the ground. We raised our guns and fired into their lines and watched as their men fell. It seemed like this went on forever. They would reload, aim, and fire. We would reload, aim, and fire, then back and forth, back and forth. Your hands would tremble."

Andrew shook his dirt-stained hands to mimic the experience.

"And it was hard to steady them while reloading. You didn't know if the powder and ball filled the barrel, and you didn't know if you'd be the next poor soul lying face down in the field. And if trying to stay alive from gunshot weren't enough, cannon balls would fly into us and explode the cavity of a man's chest on impact. Limbs were torn off, and all around us were screams. Lots of screams!"

Andrew looked up at the ceiling and laughed like a crazy man.

"But the music played on. On...and on...and damn it, it wouldn't stop! What was real? What wasn't? You couldn't tell anymore!" He looked at Nicholas like a crazy man staring back at him.

As hard as he tried, Nicholas couldn't imagine what his friend had witnessed. He had seen his own tragedies and death, but not to the scale that Andrew described. He felt sorry for him. Sorry for what he had to endure.

"No man in his right mind can tell you how war really is. We thought it was going to be glorious! Until you see it with your very eyes...and then the horror will forever be planted in your mind! Years will pass, and it will still seem like yesterday. But all was not lost that day," Andrew continued, as he relaxed a bit in his chair. "We somehow managed to repulse the attack, and Burgoyne retreated until the seventh of October. That's when we would face them again. But our spirits were high!"

Andrew sipped more coffee and thought again to himself.

"The night before the assault I left camp for the serenity of the woods, just to clear my head. The main force of the enemy, or so we thought, was encamped at a distance in front of us, since we could see the light of their fires. I wasn't too worried to venture out alone. I wandered through the woods and came upon a hill. At the top, I dropped to the ground. I saw the main force of the British army moving quietly, and I knew immediately they were preparing to flank us on the left in order to confuse and scatter us. I watched them for only a few moments as they moved cannons and wagons. Then I slithered back down the hill and ran to the officers tent to warn them. They weren't pleased that I blatantly disobeyed orders and left camp, but were grateful for the news and in no time, sent orders to regroup the majority of the men to meet the surprise attack. Unknown to Burgoyne, we were positioned heavily on his right and left. That morning he knew that his attempt to surprise us was foiled, and by the thirteenth, we had his army completely surrounded. His situation was dire, and on the seventeenth of that month he had no other recourse but to surrender."

Andrew sat back and sighed. While waiting for him to continue, Nicholas poured himself more coffee.

"For my services I was promoted to Major, since the outcome could have been disastrous had I not discovered their secret that night. But there was no celebration, since I eventually found out that the original fifteen men I enlisted with were killed in the heat of conflict. It was hard to bask in a reward when you knew that you would never see your comrades again. Yet, the promotion did give me the chance to remain in Saratoga where I met up with my father and brothers who were returning from other posts."

Andrew smiled slightly. Nicholas thought it must have been a great occasion for them to be together again.

"Our reunion was short lived, though. My father was discharged the following day and went back to the farm in New Amsterdam. The following week my brothers were sent to Cobleskill. I, being a Major, was to remain at my post and did so until the year of seventy-eight. I was at Saratoga when a dispatch delivered news of a massacre in Cobleskill on May thirtieth of the same year, and my brothers' names were listed as some of the dead."

Andrew's voice seemed to falter, and again he lowered his head so that the matted bangs of his hair almost brushed against the tabletop.

"I requested that my superior transfer me to the vicinity of Middle Fort, just south of Schoharie, so that during my service there I could somehow manage to retrieve their bodies...if not for my own satisfaction, then for that of my parents. So they could mourn peacefully, knowing that their sons were home again. I was granted permission, and when I arrived at my new station I was told by a soldier posted there that there *were* no bodies. Everyone and everything had been burned to ashes. I wanted to get home right away to give my parents the dreadful news, but remembering my orders, I stayed at the fort until late October."

Nicholas saw that Andrew was in pain and suggested he lie down a while. Andrew rejected the idea, and went on with his dreadful story as if he had to get it off his chest. Maybe after he was finished, Nicholas asked that he get some rest although, he didn't think Andrew really heard him.

"That month, Sir John Johnson—the late Major Johnson's son—appeared outside the fort with a small band of British soldiers and Mohawk Indians led by Chief Joseph Brant. They burned and pillaged the town but decided not to attack the fort, which was good for our sake, because there were only about two hundred of us and we were dangerously low on ammunition and supplies. Instead, they headed north and destroyed everything in their path. That's when I decided to leave the fort and return to my parent's farm with the understanding that I was still active and could be called back at any time to resume my post. Although the news of my brothers was tragic and unsettling, I longed to see my folks again, mostly so they wouldn't carry the burden of grieving alone. At least they would have one son home alive, and we could find closure together. That's when all hell opened up."

"Andrew, please," Nicholas said worriedly, "don't go on! I know all too well that this is difficult for you and would rather that you..."

Andrew raised his hand to quiet him.

"There's more, Nicholas," he said with an ominous look. "I'm telling you this because there's something you need to know."

Nicholas was speechless. He couldn't imagine what could possibly tie him into all of it, but gave in and sat back to let Andrew finish.

"When I reached the farm, I felt that something was terribly wrong. Things just seemed to be out of place, since it was late morning and there was no one around. My father should have been in the barn, or out in the yard as he always was at that time of day, but there wasn't the slightest hint of activity. I went to the barn to put my horse inside and saw a rotting cow, covered with flies and dried blood. There were no other animals anywhere, inside or out, but again more blood. I ran to the house and called out for Mother in vain. She too had disappeared. I checked every room, and upon reaching the kitchen I looked out through the window and into the field. My father's team was still harnessed to the plow, standing over what looked like a body, half obscured by freshly tilled ground. I ran out into the field and found him lying face up, eyes wide, looking into the sky. Blood dripped from the corner of his mouth and into the soil. I knew that it was the work of Indians because he'd been scalped."

Everything about his mother and father flooded back into Nicholas's memory, and hate flowed through him once again. He had heard at the tavern about what had happened to Andrew's father, yet didn't know what to believe until this moment. For the first time in his life, he didn't feel alone. He thought that no one on earth could understand the pain and anguish that he felt. Unfortunately, Andrew had to bear that same pain now.

"I ran to a neighbor's house and asked them if they had seen my mother. They told me she was sighted running toward the river and just vanished beyond its bank. I can only think that she fell into the water and quickly drowned. She couldn't swim, you know." Andrew's shoulders shook as he quietly sobbed.

Nicholas wanted to comfort him but couldn't. The thought of his own mother's death kept him glued to his chair. His heart ached dreadfully, and he barely realized that minutes passed before Andrew spoke again.

"After searching for hours I gave up any hope of finding her and returned to the field to bury my father. I left that night and ended up in a trading post near Caughnawaga...to sell my war horse for food, blankets, and as much ammunition as I could carry. I said to myself that whoever committed these acts would have to pay with their lives."

131

Andrew looked straight into Nicholas's eyes. "This is the part that may interest you," he said.

"I was about to leave the post when I saw a timepiece behind the counter. I made an inquiry to the proprietor that I should like to see it. The man handed it to me and right away I saw that it was my father's. I asked the man how he came of it, and he told me that four Canadian looking Indians stopped by earlier to do some trading. I asked him where they were headed and he thought north, toward Fort Johnstown. I paid for the watch with my musket and hurried to see if I could catch them. Along the way I asked if they had been spotted, and several people did confirm the suspicion that they were indeed headed in that direction. And that's how I ended up here. They are in town as we speak, probably curing their drunkenness, and I have a great hunch that they will be heading this way soon...maybe not tonight...but soon."

Nicholas knew right away what he was driving at, but could it be true?

"Andrew," Nicholas said, scratching his head, "the odds of these Indians being the same ones that..."

Again, Andrew held out his hand to interrupt him.

"There's one more thing, Nicholas, but you'll need to help me, as I am too disabled and weak."

"Of course," Nicholas replied, "anything! What do you need me to do?"

"There, next to the door, is my pack. Get it for me if you will and place it on the table."

Nicholas did as he was told and set the bag next to him. Andrew reached in the bag and while doing so said, "I haven't told you the whole story yet. I was able to make one other purchase from the trade of my horse." He pulled a pistol from the pack and laid the firearm in front of Nicholas. How strange, Nicholas thought, that Andrew would think to buy him a gift considering the circumstances. He gave Andrew a confused look.

"Pick it up, Nicholas, and tell me what you see!"

Nicholas did as Andrew asked, but didn't see anything out of the ordinary. That is, until he turned it over. On the wooden grip were the carved initials—*P. D. 1761.* Nicholas almost fell back in his chair and had to take a second look. It was there, all right…worn and barely visible…but there. It was years since he last saw his father's pistol. He always kept it on the mantle, more for show than anything else, and now Nicholas held it in his hands.

"Don't you see, Nicholas," said Andrew, "it's them! It all fits!"

Nicholas felt his stomach churn. For years he had yearned for this day to come, and now his good friend had given him the key to his salvation. Yet, he also dreaded what would have to be done.

"I can give you their description, but you have to promise me that you won't leave here on your own until I can travel with you."

Nicholas agreed, although it wasn't in earnest. After all these years of waiting, he feared missing the opportunity to settle the score.

Andrew was getting paler by the minute. Nicholas finally convinced him to lie down.

"What is the description?" asked Nicholas, sitting back in his chair after helping Andrew to his bed, then inspecting the pistol.

"I was told they have a distinct marking on their foreheads, unlike any Iroquois or Algonquin. Bluish in color…a bird or something similar. That's all I remember…but that should be enough."

Nicholas thought he remembered that the Indians who killed his parents bore a similar mark.

"Nick, be very careful tonight if you plan to go out. There is word that there will be an assault at Fort Johnstown tomorrow. There is still civil unrest in the area."

"I'll be fine. I'm staying for the night to watch over you and keep a lookout. Try to rest, and I'll have a fine meal for you when you wake."

Andrew didn't respond, as he had lost all his strength. Nicholas waited for Andrew to fall asleep before he started to make plans. He decided that he would stay the night and see to it that his friend was cared for, but in the early morning he would make the trip to the fort.

Chapter XX

Nicholas rose early, before the sun lit the sky, and before Andrew woke from his sleep. He sat at the table and penned a note to his friend in the faint light of the low burning fire.

October 25, 1781

I apologize for leaving before you could wake and stop me from being a fool. Please understand, good friend, that I've waited too long for this day to come, and am afraid that if I don't act accordingly and with haste, all hope for justice may be lost. I promise to be careful if I sense any danger along the way. If by any chance I am unsuccessful, and don't return due to my unfortunate demise, I bequeath all of my worldly things to you, since you are the closest family member I have at the present time. This being my last will and testament.

Nicholas F. Dunne

He left the letter where Andrew could easily find it and opened the door as quietly as possible. Nicholas stepped out into the dark and crossed the frozen yard. Inside the barn he loaded his musket and pistol with powder and shot and fitted Major with all of his gear. He paused only a brief moment to look back at his friend's cabin. He thought it sad that he might never see him again.

The long ride to town was uneventful until he reached the village limits. Four British guards sprang to their feet at the sight of him.

"Halt!" yelled the Sergeant, as all of them raised their guns. "State your name!"

Nicholas put his hands in the air and brought Major to a stop.

"The name is Nicholas Dunne," he said. "I have pelts to trade, so that I might get a meal and drink at the tavern."

The Sergeant and one of the other soldiers kept their muskets on him, while the other two rushed to the side of his horse.

"Dismount from your horse, sir, and be quick about it," the Sergeant demanded.

Nicholas did as he was told. The soldiers shoved him away from Major and searched through his property.

"Some pelts, a loaded musket and pistol. Nothing else of importance," one of the soldiers yelled back.

"Search him for any dispatch papers," he ordered.

Nicholas kept his hands in the air and made sure not to make any sudden movements. They searched his person and made their report.

"Everything seems to be in order."

The Sergeant lowered his musket and instructed the other men to surround Nicholas with their bayonets. He approached Nicholas and gave him a suspicious look, before rummaging through his pack.

"Why are your weapons loaded?" he inquired.

"I always keep ready so that if I come across some game worth taking, I can get off a quick shot. The animals of the forest are my livelihood, which I'm sure a man of honor, such as yourself, wouldn't deny, would he not, sir?"

The Sergeant walked around him, eyeing him up and down. "Why the pistol?" he asked in a sneering tone. "It seems to me that an experienced woodsman like yourself would only need one good shot. Certainly a pistol wouldn't be of much use...would it?"

"A man whose sight begins to wane from his eyes, such as myself, is surely to miss his mark, sir. A man with good vision may only need one shot to my two." Nicholas responded. He hoped the lie sounded genuine enough to fool them.

"I see," he said with skepticism. "Then a man with nothing to hide has no worry. Am I right, Mr. Dunne?"

Nicholas didn't respond, feeling he had already said enough.

The Sergeant stared at him to see if Nicholas would unravel. But he didn't. Still, the Sergeant wasn't satisfied in the least, and he turned toward two of the soldiers and barked, "Take him to the jail for further questioning!"

The soldiers grabbed his arms and Nicholas gave in without

resistance.

"We shall see if you are telling the truth," he said, as the soldiers whisked away their captive.

Nicholas was immediately delivered to the jailhouse and placed in a cell, until an officer had him released and brought into a small room. He was ordered to sit, his wrists secured tightly behind his back. A soldier stood guard at the door.

The officer in charge walked toward him, his hands folded behind his back. "Your name?" he demanded with authority.

"Nicholas Dunne."

The man walked to his right and turned.

"At the present, what is your residence, Mr. Dunne?"

"North of here," replied Nicholas, "near Fifth Lake."

"Near the vicinity of the Garoga lakes?" the officer said, walking in front of him.

"A few miles or so."

The officer snapped his fingers and the guard approached with some papers.

"Do you know a man named..." He paused to scan the papers. "Ah, here it is," he continued, "one, Andrew Smith?" then looked back at Nicholas.

"I have heard the name, but he is no acquaintance of mine, sir," said Nicholas, swallowing hard. "I keep to myself."

"I'm finding it difficult to believe that at some time or another, you would not know who your neighbors are," the officer said, "especially, since a man of your trade would find it necessary to cover some distance in the wilderness."

"If you please, sir, what I say is the truth. I am but a humble man and only know his name, except for the fact that his dwelling has been abandoned for years and that he is feared dead. So it is said."

The officer walked over to the soldier, handed him the papers, and with his back to Nicholas prodded, "Do you know why you're here, Mr. Dunne?"

Nicholas thought that he was found out, but kept steady and replied, "I do not, sir."

Turning back to him, the officer said, "We have intercepted papers near New Amsterdam from a dispatch rider who carried for the

Continental Army...and in those papers was the request that a Major Andrew Smith report back for immediate duty. Two evenings ago we were informed that there was an individual resembling your appearance, with a similar name, who seemed to be interested in a tragedy that occurred on a farm where this, Smith family resides," he said with some distaste, looking down at Nicholas to see if he had struck a nerve. "We also have information regarding his last known residence, but, unfortunately, I cannot afford to send any of my men to the Garoga area. And since you reside within the approximate location in question, you can understand my concern. Therefore, due to the circumstances, I would like to know your whereabouts on the day of the twenty-third."

"I can assure you sir, that this is the first trip I've made from the mountains in perhaps a month or so," said Nicholas. "Like I said from the beginning, and with all due respect, sir, I prefer to keep to myself as much as I'm allowed. I'm just a poor trapper and seek nothing else than to make an honest living."

"Yes, that *is* similar to what you said before," the officer said lightly, leaning back on his heels. "Or so it's what you claim."

The officer paced the room a few times, and then stepped toward the guard. He softly spoke to him and the guard abruptly departed. Turning back to Nicholas, he said, "I have sent word to locate the two patrons that frequented the tavern on that day. I'm sure you have no objection to remaining here a bit longer for identification purposes, do you, Mr. Dunne?"

"If it pleases you, sir," said Nicholas. "My only wish is to clear my name and set your mind at ease."

"We shall see," the officer replied.

The door burst open and the guard reappeared.

"Sir, there is confirmation that the American forces are within one mile to the southeast! I have been directed to send for your immediate return to Major Ross's quarters."

The officer instantly stepped toward the door.

"Sir," said the guard, "what about the prisoner?"

The officer turned and looked at Nicholas for a moment. "I don't believe this man has committed any serious crime," he said. "Release him at once. And Mr. Dunne, on my advice, you are to gather your things and leave this area immediately! Are we clear?" he sternly demanded.

"Yes, sir," said Nicholas, rubbing his wrists after he was untied.

Nicholas let out a huge sigh of relief as the men exited the room.

Outside the jail, Major was tied up and waiting for him. He briskly walked down the steps and inadvertently bumped into a man who was on his way up.

"Pardon," said the man as he glanced at Nicholas.

Nicholas froze in his tracks and looked back. The man stopped at the top step and also turned, his eyes widening. Nicholas saw that it was one of the men he had talked to in the tavern.

"Wait a minute," the man yelled, pointing a finger, "I know you! You're the one who..."

But before he could finish, Nicholas leapt on his horse and rode away as fast as Major could gallop. He turned down a side street and headed for the forest. He could hear the man screaming for the guards even as he reached the edge of the woods.

After a minute or two had passed, Nicholas realized that he wasn't being tailed and let Major rest. Through the trees, he saw British soldiers running toward the other edge of town at the beat of a drum. Keeping his distance from the edge of the forest, he rode to the south and discovered an army of Continental soldiers moving rapidly toward the field beyond the town's limits. He found a safe place to hold up and watched in awe as the two armies formed their lines. He heard fifes playing in unison with the rapid beat of snare drums and understood what Andrew meant about the music. The tune of the fifes and drums set an eerie mood. Then, just as abruptly, everything went silent.

Chapter XXI

Nicholas nudged Major to the edge of the woods overlooking the center of the field. He could plainly hear officers from both sides barking orders from the back of their lines, as their horses galloped to and fro. To rapid drumbeats, men scurried into position. The officers anxiously barked out more orders, and cannon on both sides rang out.

Major reared as the first cannonball exploded dead center in the field, sending rock and dirt for yards. Soon after, more shots found their mark. The drums and fifes started playing again, and the two forces marched toward one another, flags held high in the center of their lines. When they were only about fifty yards apart, a rapid beat was sounded and the British soldiers leveled their muskets. At an officer's command, a great volley of musket fire erupted with flames and smoke.

Some of the Continental soldiers dropped to the ground and lay motionless. The others stood like statues, their muskets held vertically. A second order was sounded and the Continentals lowered their muskets and fired into the enemy's lines. After each volley, the lines advanced a little further and fired again. This went on until both armies were in range of being cut down by cannon fire.

The soldiers fixed bayonets to the ends of their muskets and charged one another. Nicholas couldn't imagine Andrew experiencing the carnage that was playing out before him first hand. What a waste that so many men would die, he thought, as the hand-to-hand combat raged within yards of him.

From out of nowhere and without warning, four Indians streaked past him, hugging the edge of the field and whooping in short yelps. Within seconds they tackled an American soldier and sunk a hatchet into his chest. The man screamed as he was clubbed about the head. One of the warriors scalped him, while the other three scavenged through his clothes.

The warrior holding the dead man's scalp looked into the woods. Nicholas saw the faint blue paint on his forehead and reached for his musket. The Indian simultaneously grabbed for the American's musket. Major pranced about as Nicholas tried to get a clear and steady shot through the trees.

The Indian unloaded his round, which ricocheted off the tree directly in front of Nicholas. He finally found an optimum moment and pulled back the hammer. Just as he squeezed the trigger, he felt something sock him in his midsection, and a bolt of white light flashed in his eyes. His gun tipped downward and fired next to Major's head. The horse kicked its hind legs and leapt into the clearing. Major jumped over the dead soldier, nearly trampling the Indian warrior, and raced along the back of the American line.

Nicholas held Major's neck to keep from falling, screaming with pain each time the horse's hooves struck the ground. Major covered more than three quarters of the field before a shell exploded nearby. He reared up with a great whinny and Nicholas was thrown to the ground. The scared horse danced around wildly before galloping full steam into the thick of the battle.

"Major, NO!" Nicholas screamed in desperation. He got to his feet, gripping the arrow that protruded through his coat, and dashed for the opposite end of the field. But the pain was too much and he fell to the ground. He looked back to see if he was being followed, but could only see traces of red and blue figures clashing violently.

Again he rose to his feet and ran toward the woods. With any luck at all, he could get into the cover of the trees and remain hidden.

Nicholas reached the edge of the woods, only to find a rock wall three feet high blocking his escape route. He rolled over the wall on his good side, suffering a great deal of pain. Once on the other side of the barrier, he lay on his back in the musty leaves and as close to the wall as possible, contemplating his next move.

He lifted his head and saw the arrow rise and fall with each breath. It must have been a stray shot that somehow managed to find him. It looked like a Mohawk arrow, and strangely, he thought he had seen the type of arrow once before. The feathers were brightly colored, and there were four instead of the usual three. In a flash, and oddly enough, his mind wandered back to Andrew.

Nicholas thought of the note he had written him before he left the cabin. It was disheartening to think of how he might have let his friend down, and that if he were to die, all of their unfinished business of revenge might never come to fruition. He wished that he had taken Andrew's advice and waited. Even if they never caught up with the Indians, at least he would still be alive.

He thought of Tawanda, his only true love. Now he would probably never see her again. He would lose the only woman who ever cared for him. He wasn't worried about her being cared for. Manendra would see to that. He thought about just giving in and dying right there. That way he could end the mental anguish that had haunted him for what seemed like an eternity. And, he could stop hurting the ones he cared about as well.

Light from the early sun pierced through the dense fog, somehow calming him. He watched the tall trees sway in the breeze and felt like he was floating. He didn't feel the pain anymore and closed his eyes. Except for the breeze, all the sounds around him grew distant; the boom of the cannon, men screaming, the crackle of musket-fire—all was unreal to him now. The calm breeze brushed his face as he lay in silence, until the ground under him shook.

Nicholas tensed up and opened his eyes. He heard horses on the opposite side of the wall. He sat up and winced. The arrow shifted as he painstakingly rose to his feet. He couldn't bear the thought of losing his hair to a savage without, at least, giving them a good fight.

He went deeper into the woods and paused to rest against a tree. If he had enough strength to make it back to town, he might be able to locate a doctor to help save him. He had to keep moving, but first he had to rest for just a few more moments.

That was the last he remembered.

Part III

Nicholas – The Warrior

The bitter end of revenge

Chapter XXII

Nicholas opened his eyes a little and saw the tops of the trees brushing against the bright blue sky. They swayed gently in the breeze as they slowly passed him by. His body bounced on the angled stretcher as he was dragged through the woods. He tried to understand where he was, but his mind swirled with confusion. He might have thought he had died, if not for the sharp and deliberate pain that plagued his side.

Placing his hands on the wooden framework, he used all his might to pull himself up. He barely raised himself an inch before falling back with a terrible weakness that made him feel faint. As much as he struggled to keep awake, it was no use. Nicholas reluctantly closed his eyes.

Sometime later he awoke. He was someplace very familiar. It was dark except for a fire close by. He could hear low voices inside the structure where he lay, and thought that he could make out some images sitting in a circle across the room. His memory started to filter back and he recognized the longhouse that he once called home.

"It was all a dream," he thought to himself, still quite dazed.

He couldn't understand why he was so tired. He tried to get out of bed before anyone realized he was awake. He knew that the women would give him a good scolding if he didn't get outside with the other boys. Just as he lifted himself, a searing pain streamed through his body and he let out a short scream.

Nicholas held his side and could barely breathe. He managed to slowly lie back down. Visions came and went, making him feel sick to his stomach. It felt like all the blood had drained from his body. In an instant his skin became cold and clammy.

"Do not try to get up," a woman said to him. "You are still very weak and must not use your strength."

The woman's voice was very pleasing to Nicholas and strangely recognizable. He half-opened his eyes and saw the profile of a beautiful young Indian woman kneeling next to him. He felt her soft hands lightly touch his skin as she tugged and pressed gently on his side.

"Where..." he barely uttered. His voice was raspy and he couldn't get out another word.

"Don't speak," the woman quietly ordered. "You need to rest, White Bear."

He wondered how this beautiful woman knew who he was. And before he could analyze his situation any further, he fell back into a deep, quiet sleep.

As Nicholas came to, he heard water dripping into a bowl and felt a wet cloth gently pat his side. The muffled laughs of children and the constant bark of a dog came from outside. He stirred a little and saw that the young woman was again kneeling next to him with a wooden bowl and washrag. She smiled at him when she dipped the cloth into the water and rung it out, looking almost angelic in the soft light. He thought that she was the most beautiful woman he had ever seen. Her long, black hair was tied in a braid that hung nearly to the floor. Her face was olive-colored and smooth, with high cheekbones. He had seen her before, but couldn't quite make out where or when.

"You're awake!" she said with surprise, raising her eyebrows. "Are you thirsty or hungry?"

Nicholas struggled to get out some words. "Thirsty," he croaked.

She placed the cloth in the bowl and carried it across the room, returning with a flask and cup. She knelt and gently lifted his head so she could place the rim of the cup on his lips. Nicholas let the cool liquid stream into his mouth and coughed as it reached the back of his throat. He sat up a little and she held him until he could clear his lungs.

"Do not try to drink so much," she said, again placing the cup to his lips. This time, he let a little water pool in his mouth before swallowing.

"Where am I?" he said, looking around as far as his head could turn.

"You are in our village, White Bear...where you once lived."

Nicholas looked puzzled and said, "You know my name that was given to me years ago...and you look familiar to me. What is your name?"

She smiled at him, and it dawned on Nicholas who she might be. But the girl he knew years ago was not a woman...

Nicholas feebly placed a hand on her arm. "Tawanda?"

"It is me, Nicholas," she said lovingly.

"My God, you are beautiful!" he exclaimed, holding her with as much strength as he could muster.

"And you are still with fever, or so you must be," she said, blushing. She placed a cool hand on his forehead.

"I thought I would never see you again," he said. "You have to believe me when I tell you..."

"Shhh. We will have plenty of time to talk. But now you must rest. I will get you something to eat. You have lost a lot of blood and need to regain your strength."

There were so many questions that buzzed through Nicholas's head. The last thing he could remember was his cabin in Garoga and getting ready to harvest the vegetables he had grown. He couldn't understand how he ended up in the village so many miles away. But his mind went back to Tawanda and how good it was to be with her again, even if things were all a blur. If he couldn't remember his past, maybe she or someone else could help him piece it all together.

Tawanda was back with another bowl, only this time it was filled with food. The aroma of meat and corn made his stomach growl. Soon after he finished eating, he fell fast asleep. But it wasn't a sound sleep. His fever had come back with a vengeance and his dreams were filled with bits and pieces of his mother and father and the faces of everyone he knew in his lifetime. None of it made any sense. It was as if many events were all balled up and resurfacing all at once. He was relieved to have woken from his slumber and find that his fever had subsided.

As expected, Tawanda was next to him that morning. She had kept a cool, damp cloth on his head the whole night as he tossed and turned.

"Your fever has broken," she said, as Nicholas tried to keep his heavy eyelids open. She gave him more liquid to drink, which instantly quenched his dry mouth and throat.

"How long have I been here?" he asked. He was feeling better, even though he was still very weak.

"Eight days," she said.

"What happened?" asked Nicholas, trying to raise himself up on his side. "I mean, the last I remember is my cabin...or a battle...or something," he said, rubbing his head. Nicholas winced when his hand touched the healing gash next to his temple.

"Father brought you here. He found you in the woods during the great battle. You were struck by an arrow and it was removed the night that you came. I don't know any more than what I was told."

"The battle?" questioned Nicholas, trying hard to remember. "I do remember something about a battle. Where did it take place?"

"Fort Johnstown," said Tawanda, checking his side. "The Americans came from the southern pass and met the red-coated soldiers and our people in a field. Father found you in the woods when the men were fighting. He saw that you were badly hurt and didn't know if you would live."

Some things started to come back to Nicholas. He seemed to remember the battle that Tawanda talked about, but the details of everything before and after were mostly a large void.

"What became of the Americans and British?"

"The Americans drove them to the west. Father was disappointed because the war is over for the Mohawk people. He decided that enough of our braves were lost and that to continue fighting would not be wise, for fear that it could be the end of our people. Father can tell you more when you are well enough to sit before council."

Nicholas saw that she was distraught.

"What's wrong, Tawanda?" he asked, but she looked away and wouldn't say anything. Nicholas turned her face so she would have to look at him. "What is it that you're not telling me?"

Looking into his eyes, Tawanda reluctantly told him his fate.

"As soon as you're well, you will stand trial before council for your crimes," she said sadly.

"Crimes!" exclaimed Nicholas. "I know of no crimes that I committed! I can't remember anything as of yet, but I'm sure that I wouldn't have done any injustice toward your father...my father," he corrected himself, "and certainly not toward the Mohawk people! I don't understand!"

Tawanda took a deep breath. "Even though Father is chief, he cannot disobey the laws that we live by. As of now, Nicholas, you are being held as a prisoner for treason!"

"Treason!" he cried. "What treason?"

Tawanda looked away and didn't want to say any more than she had. Nicholas gripped her wrist hard and pleaded, "Tawanda, treason for what?"

"They believe that you were fighting with the Americans!" she blurted. "But you are alive because Father keeps you alive! He has told only me that he doesn't believe what the others say, but if it's true and you are found guilty, the punishment is death!" Tears rolled down her cheeks. "Nicholas," she begged, "I don't believe them either, but you must find a way to remember what happened that day. If I lose you again, I too should rather die than walk soul-less upon the earth!"

Nicholas loosened his grip on her and lay down. Tawanda was right. He had to somehow remember all that he could to save himself. He knew in his heart that whatever had happened, he could never have done anything so despicable to alienate himself from his own kind.

"Because Father is one of the three chiefs, he will help you as much as he can, yet there is only so much that he will be able to do. You must defend yourself and remember as much as you can!" Tawanda pleaded.

Nicholas turned his head away. His situation at the moment looked grim and he couldn't bear losing everything again—Tawanda, justice for his parents, his good friend Andrew, his life. Nicholas sat up with excitement and lost his breath as his side gave him great pain.

"That's it!" he said, grimacing. "Andrew! Oh dear God, I left Andrew!" All that was forgotten rushed back to him with a frenzy. He pushed at Tawanda's shoulder and said, "Quick, find Manendra and ask him if he will see me! I remember!"

Tawanda wiped the tears from her face and looked at him with doubt.

"Go!" he urged, as he pushed her again.

She jumped to her feet and ran out of the longhouse. Nicholas lay back down and tried to piece it all together and eventually remembered everything.

Within minutes, Tawanda and Manendra appeared and stood

149

over Nicholas. Manendra knelt down and looked gravely into his eyes.

"What do you remember?" Manendra said calmly.

"Enough!" said Nicholas.

"You must be sure of yourself, my son."

"I'm more certain now than I'll ever be," Nicholas assured him.

Manendra looked at him for a long moment to make sure he wasn't still delirious. When he saw that Nicholas was coherent, he stood up and said, "Then it is time. I will assemble the council and you will be brought to us when the sun leaves the sky."

Tawanda sat next to him and held his hand. Nicholas looked deep into her eyes with a smile and gently squeezed her hand, as they waited together for dusk to come.

Chapter XXIII

An Indian brave entered the longhouse and helped Tawanda lift Nicholas onto his weak legs. They led him to the longhouse where the council of the three chiefs were waiting. Tawanda wasn't allowed to enter. Only the brave could help him inside and sit him in front of the low burning fire pit. Manendra sat on the opposite side of him, with the two other chiefs to his right and a warrior to his left. Nicholas recognized the warrior as his step-brother Alok, who seemingly had changed very little with age.

Alok didn't look at him. Instead, he stared straight ahead, as motionless as a statue.

Manendra and the other chiefs huddled together and whispered to each other before Manendra began the proceedings. Nicholas barely heard Manendra speak, as the pain in his side made it difficult.

"You claim to be White Bear of the Turtle, a name that was given to you with my own breath," Manendra said. "If one claims to be who he says he is, then there must be proof. If the one is proven to be him, then council will question him to see if he has committed unlawful things against the people of the Mohawk. If the one cannot prove who he says he is, then he will be punished with death. If the one proves to be who he says, but cannot prove his innocence, then he will also receive the same punishment."

Manendra and the chiefs leaned into each other and once again spoke with low words so that Nicholas couldn't hear what they were saying. Manendra sat up straight and continued to speak.

"If the accused proves to council that he is White Bear of the Turtle, and satisfies council that no crimes against the people of the Mohawk have been committed, then he is free to go and be at peace with the people of the Mohawk."

"What is the name that you are called by the white man?" questioned one of the chiefs.

"I am called Nicholas Dunne," he said in fluent Mohawk, trying desperately to ward off the pain for fear that he might faint and cause the trial to come to an abrupt end.

"What are the names of your parents who gave you that name?" asked the same chief.

"My father was Patrick Dunne. My mother was Catherine with the same last name as my father. They lived on the land where I was born…land that lies to the north near the lakes of Garoga. It is land that I have reclaimed as my property."

"How were you given the name White Bear, and what proof do you have?" said the second chief.

"The name was given to me by Manendra, Chief of the Turtle Clan. My parents were murdered and Manendra, my Indian father, adopted me into the tribe. Since then, eight harvests have passed."

"You say that you are White Bear, yet any man can give himself a name and steal the identity of another," said the first chief. "What else can you offer us, so that we may see the truth in what you say?"

Nicholas slid up his sleeve to expose his forearm. Manendra watched him in silence. Nicholas held up his arm to show them a T-shaped scar.

"This is the mark that I received when I was young," said Nicholas. "The man who was once called Major Johnson, and friend to the people of the Mohawk, held a great meeting for all tribes of the Iroquois. There was a great celebration of peace, and there were many events for the Indian and English boys to compete in. I entered into a wrestling game with another boy from the Wolf Clan and, to his dismay, proved my strength. He grew angry with me and pulled a knife from his sheath, and cut me before I could wrestle him to the ground."

"These are lies!" shouted Alok, even though he knew Nicholas was telling the truth. "The one that sits before you tries to fool you with a crooked tongue, like his kind have done in the past to sway the Mohawk. This only proves that he aims to outwit the council to save his own skin. He is a master of trickery and his words cannot be trusted," he said, glaring at Nicholas. "Ask him for other proof, as he has not shown council evidence to spare his life!"

Manendra let his son rant and waited for the other chiefs to question him more thoroughly.

"If you are Nich-o-las Dunne, son of the white man named Patrick, adopted son of Manendra," said the first chief, "then you would know things that only he and his adopted father would know. Can you tell us these things?"

Nicholas knew what they wanted to hear and slid his sleeve back over his arm.

"Manendra, my adopted father and Chief of the Turtle Clan, goes by another name that was given to him as a boy...by a great man that was known to all of the Mohawk and Iroquois people," Nicholas said, looking at Manendra. "The English one called William Johnson had saved the life of an Indian infant many, many seasons ago. He found the small child underneath the body of his mother who, with an entire village, was slaughtered by their northern brothers, the Algonquins. He took the boy infant, named him Joseph, and gave him over to the Mohawk, so that he would be protected and could live and learn the ways of his people. The boy Joseph, became the great chief known as Manendra. My parents knew this, and now I am the only white man left who knows. These are the things that the chief, called Manendra, told to me."

Alok jumped up with rage, pointed at Nicholas, and shouted, "Lies! I am the son of the great Chief Manendra and do not know this, so it is not the truth!" Alok looked at Manendra and said, "Do we have to listen to any more of this? Now we know that he tells stories and is mad with confusion."

Manendra held up his hand so that Alok would sit back down. They were all looking at him, waiting for a response. Nicholas didn't want to expose the secret that Manendra had held onto for a very long time, and thought that the he *could* deny Nicholas's every word.

After a brief silence, Manendra finally spoke, never looking away from Nicholas.

"It is true that I was given a Christian name by the white leader John-son. It is also true that the name given to me was Jo-seph. The one called Nich-o-las Dunne by the white man, and known as White Bear to the Mohawk, *is* the only one to know this."

The two chiefs leaned close to one another and whispered. Alok grew anxious and couldn't believe what he was hearing. He knew that his father was convinced that the man before them was his step-brother, but Alok wasn't quite through with him yet. There was still the matter of siding with the enemy.

"Even if he is who he claims, there is still the question of whether or not he fights alongside our enemy," said Alok. "The one called White Bear was seen to have raised his weapon in the time of battle to slay a brother warrior. It is the truth that the bluecoats did not side with any of our brothers that day or the English! Surely that proves to council that he must be an ally to the Americans!"

The three chiefs again whispered to each other.

"It has been proven to the council that he who is on trial before us is the one that is known as White Bear," said the chief. "The council has also listened to the argument of Alok, head of the Mohawk warriors. His father, who is Chief Manendra, also confirms that the one seen with his weapon raised against our brother is the one who sits before us. Do you deny any of this?"

"No," said Nicholas. "I do not deny that I had placed the sights of my gun to the breast of an Indian man, and I do not deny that the same Indian is my enemy."

Alok was surprised that Nicholas was giving in so easily. Surely he would be found guilty now, but by his own words and not through Alok's accusations.

"Yet, the same Indian man you call a brother is no ally to the Mohawk people," continued Nicholas. "They are renegades cast out from their own tribe and live within the French territories of Canada. They wear the mark of the flying bird, with the left tip of the wing at their left temple and the right tip of the wing at their right temple, and joined together at the center of their forehead. On the battlefield, I watched them take the life of an American, same as I watched them as a boy take the lives of my parents. I watched them claim the scalp and possessions of the American soldier as they also did to my parents. I was not there to fight the warriors of the Mohawk or their English allies, or the Americans. I was there to kill for my own personal reasons."

"Again, he does not speak the truth!" cried Alok. "He spins a web of lies to turn brother against brother. This is not the way that..."

"Enough!" barked Manendra. "He tells the truth. I, too, have seen with my own eyes the warriors of which he speaks. Twice I have seen the mark that is carried on their forehead. The first time was when his parents' lives were taken…and the second in battle. What good would it do him to lie?" Manendra looked directly at Alok. "If two brothers went fishing, and one brother was jealous and secretly conspired to rid himself of the other brother, and when only one returned to tell the people of his misfortune, would that not be a crime against all people? You speak of words of turning brother against brother. But before you speak of any other words, it is wise to seek the truth in your own heart first, and then decide whether those words should pass from your lips."

Alok looked at Manendra in shock. How had his father known about what happened at the river so long ago? Defeated and humiliated, Alok kept silent throughout the rest of the trial.

The chiefs whispered for a long while before reaching a decision.

"The council has decided to free White Bear of all charges, since no crimes against the Mohawk Nation have been proven," said the first chief. "White Bear will remain in the house of Chief Manendra until he is well. Then, he is to leave and never return to the lands of the Mohawk."

Nicholas was glad that his life was spared, yet to be banned forever was disheartening. He would probably never see Manendra or Tawanda again. Even Andrew's friendship would hardly make up for his losses.

An Indian brave was summoned to take him back to the longhouse. Tawanda was waiting for him outside. Nicholas placed his arm around her shoulder. Because he had lost a lot of energy, he quickly passed out in his bed once he reached the longhouse. Tawanda was told by her father that his life had been spared, but that he would have to leave when he was able. She was not sad at the news. Instead, Tawanda made preparations for that time to come.

That evening, Nicholas woke and talked with Tawanda. He told her what happened and what would become of him. He told her how much he loved her and found it very hard to think that he would probably never see her again. She wouldn't talk about it, and he assumed that it hurt her too much. After all, they would only have a week or so together before he was well enough to set out on his own again.

The night before Nicholas was well enough to leave, he sat alone by the fire when Manendra approached him. Manendra brought him the things that were picked up on the battlefield, which Nicholas thought he had lost forever.

"You will need these on your journey home," said Manendra, placing Nicholas's musket, pistol, and knife next to him.

Nicholas was relieved to have them again. "Thank you," he said solemnly. "How did you find out about the fishing trip?"

"Tawanda didn't know I was awake when she threatened her brother in the dark. The next day we spoke, and she told me what had happened, and I vowed to her that I would keep her words inside me. It is the only vow I have ever broken."

Manendra stared into the fire, then looked at his adopted son.

"I only hope that you see that Alok does have a good heart. I know this of my son, but he has not realized it yet. In time he will. You, on the other hand, have always acted with your heart, and it is my fault that I have thought of you differently than him. I know now that I caused Alok to feel like you were the important one, although this was not what I intended."

Nicholas knew what he meant and couldn't imagine what might have become of him if Manendra *hadn't* shown him the attention and affection he needed during those tender times. He supposed that Alok was right to be jealous and displeased.

"I do wish the best for him," said Nicholas, looking down. "I am the jealous one. He will always have his father and I will have lost two."

"You can't lose what's in your heart, White Bear. We are together in spirit, in life, and will be so in death. This is what we are grateful for. But now you must concentrate on life, so that you will be satisfied in death."

"I can never repay you, Father, for all you've given me," Nicholas said earnestly.

Manendra gazed back into the fire. "I never thought I could repay Major Johnson for my life, but I know now that it was wrong to think that way." Manendra put his hand on Nicholas's shoulder. "You will always be my son, and that is payment enough." With that,

156

Manendra stood to leave.

"I will always be there if you need me, Father," Nicholas said.

"I know, my son," Manendra said from the entrance of the longhouse. "There will be a horse ready for you before the sun rises." He gave Nicholas an affectionate look before leaving the longhouse.

Nicholas picked up his things, got up from the fire, and went over to his bed to sleep in great sadness.

Chapter XXIV

Tawanda was not in her bed when Nicholas went to say goodbye to her. He was relieved in a way, since seeing her would be too painful. He thought that she must have felt the same. He wished that he had given her something to remember him by, although it was easier this way. Maybe she would find another man to love and, more importantly, a man that would love her back. Someone she could bear children with Nicholas thought, as he packed his things and stepped out into the cool morning air.

As promised by Manendra, a horse waited for him next to the longhouse. To his surprise, Tawanda sat on a second horse staring straight ahead and pretended not to notice him.

"Why are you here?" he said.

"I am going with you," she said.

"Tawanda, you cannot go with me. It's too dangerous."

"If I cannot go with you, then I will go elsewhere," she said firmly.

"Where would you go? Your family is here. I cannot provide for you, and you would not be safe by yourself!"

She looked down at him, holding the reins with a tight grip.

"You do not need to provide for me. I can do that for the both of us. I will not see you go away from me again. When you left the first time, my heart was full of sorrow and I lost my soul. I was only able to accept life because I hoped that one day I would see you again."

"Tawanda, please don't..."

Tawanda held up her hand and said, "Please let me finish. I cannot live anymore without you, Nicholas. I love you. I've always loved you. If you do not love me, then I will understand, but I will still leave because I cannot stay. I have shamed my people by not having a husband and children as I am expected. Mostly, I have shamed my father."

Nicholas knew she was right. The Mohawk depended on their

women to bear as many children as possible to keep their bloodline strong. He would have tried harder to talk her out of it, but knew it would have been no use. Besides, he loved her as well, and wanted her to go with him even if the risk was great.

"Please, Nicholas, don't leave me if you do care for me," she pleaded. "You will see that I am strong-willed and a good companion. I will give you children and take care of you. This is my promise."

Nicholas knew he would give in to her, but there were still so many doubts.

"What about Manendra? Even if I agree to let you accompany me, I would have to know if he permits it."

"Father knows of my wishes and gives us his approval. He has given me gifts to show you how he feels. He knew that you would not take me with you without having his permission first." She reached into a leather bag strapped to the horse. "This is for you," she said, handing him a carved pipe decorated with feathers. "It is the pipe of a chief. It is Manendra's."

Nicholas took the pipe and looked it over. It was definitely a sacred piece and by right should only be in the possession of a high-ranking Mohawk.

"This is what Father gave to me," she said, pulling a necklace from under her coat.

It was no ordinary necklace. It was decorated with the finest beads, shells, and stones, worthy of an Indian princess.

"You see?" said Tawanda. "These things, and the horses, are wedding gifts. It is Father's wish. If you do not agree with this, then we will ride together until we are far away from the village. Then we can go separate ways, and no one will know that we have parted."

Nicholas looked up at her and squeezed her hand tightly.

"I love you more than anything! And because I love you, you may be with me only on the condition that you do as I say, go where I go, and live as I live. This is only for your safety. There will surely be danger in our path and we must be prepared. No harm will come to you from the Americans, as long as you stay close to me at all times. Do you understand what I'm telling you?"

Tawanda nodded. Nicholas pulled the pistol from his belt and gave it to her. "Do you know how to use this?" he asked.

"Yes. It has been a long time, but I still remember."

"Keep it hidden in the pack at all times, unless I tell you to use it...or if something happens to me and you need to use it in self-defense. This is very important, Tawanda! Any Indian, whether it be a man, woman, or child, caught with a weapon by the Americans will surely be imprisoned or executed. As long as you are close by my side, you will not need to worry. Understand?"

"Yes, Nicholas. I understand."

"Good," he said, and mounted his horse. "Then we should go. Keep your horse close to mine and do not speak. Watch me at all times for signals of danger. We won't be out of harm's way until we reach the north pass beyond Fort Johnstown."

Nicholas and Tawanda left the village and didn't look back. For some strange reason, Nicholas was afraid he might see Manendra standing with his arm in the air. Yet he knew that would not be the case. And he knew that he would never see Manendra again.

Tawanda did as Nicholas instructed and kept her horse close to his. Before they reached the outskirts of town he got down from his horse, took a leather strap from his pack, and went over to her.

"Give me your wrists," he said.

Tawanda held them out and he tied them loosely together with the strap.

"This is for your protection," he said. "I'm sure by now that the Americans have taken the town, and as long as they think you're my hostage, you won't be bothered. The straps are loose enough for you to slip out of if you need to do so. Otherwise, keep your wrists together and do not speak to me or anyone. I need to visit the tavern in town to see if there is any news. I won't be long inside, so just stay with the horses."

Tawanda nodded and Nicholas took her reins. He hopped back on his horse and it wasn't long before they entered the town.

The square was bustling with activity when they arrived, and many American soldiers were all about. Aside from a few stares directed toward their way, no one paid them too much attention. It wasn't unusual for a stranger to enter town with an Indian captive. In fact, it was allowed by proclamation, as long as there was no immediate threat to the townspeople. And because Tawanda's wrists appeared to be bound, there was no need for anyone to be concerned.

Nicholas stopped in front of the tavern where many men were gathered, and left Tawanda with the horses tied to a post. He gave her a quick glance to see if she was too nervous to be left alone, and relaxed when he saw that she sat very still.

He entered the building, went straight to the bar, and ordered a drink. He stood next to a bulky man who was leaning over the bar, drinking a beer. The man's coat was made from bear, and his coyote hat and scraggly beard covered most of his face. Nicholas raised his glass.

"I've been away for a bit and was wondering, friend, if there was any news," Nicholas said nonchalantly, sipping his drink.

The man didn't acknowledge him, and Nicholas thought that the trapper didn't realize he was being addressed. Nicholas turned slightly toward the fellow and tried a second time to strike up a conversation.

"Pardon me, friend, but I said that I've been away and..."

"I heard you the first time, boy," the man grumbled. "Maybe it would be wise if you tended to your own affairs and left me be." He opened his coat to expose a large knife in his waist belt.

The man took one last gulp of his beer, slammed the mug down, and tossed a coin on the bar. He intentionally knocked into Nicholas as he staggered toward the door. Nicholas calmly took another sip of whiskey.

"Don't mind him," a patron said to Nicholas. "That's just Pete's way of introducing himself. For the most part, his stink is the most harm he's done around here. Name's Robert Stack," the man said with a smile and held out his hand. "Most just call me Bob. And you are?"

Nicholas put down his glass and shook his hand. "Name's Ni..." he began, then caught himself. "Nickerson. Patrick Nickerson."

"Well, Patrick Nickerson, how about another...on me?" the cheerful man said, slapping some coins on the bar.

"I appreciate the hospitality, but I just came in to catch up on any news of the war before I head back to the mountains."

"Not much to tell, except that the Americans and French have the British in a bottleneck," he said, swirling the liquor in his glass before taking a drink. He winced as the drink went down hard. "Never could get used to cheap rot gut. As I was saying, most believe that the war will be over soon. It's over for us, anyway. The American and French forces are pushing the main army of the redcoats further to the south. Some of us that live outside of town, which I'm assuming you're from, only have to worry about the savages."

Nicholas lowered his glass to the bar. "How so?" he said, trying to be discreet.

"Every now and then, there's word that a settler will have to fend 'em off from stealin' their livestock. And if they're lucky enough to catch one, he can turn 'em in to the authorities for payment. The unfortunate ones that get caught are usually hung. If it's a woman or child, then they can be sold for hard labor."

Nicholas lifted his glass to his mouth and pretended this news didn't bother him.

"Like Pete, for example," the man said, pointing with his glass toward the front window. "I'm sure the Indian woman he just left with will bring him a good share of silver."

Nicholas turned and saw that Tawanda was gone. He dropped his glass and bolted for the door.

"Where ya goin', friend?" the man cried. "Didn't get a chance to buy ya one yet!"

Nicholas frantically scoured the street for any sign of them and started to panic. He leapt on his horse and grabbed the reins of Tawanda's. At the east end of the street he noticed a barn door slightly ajar and thought he heard a muffled scream.

Racing to the barn, he jumped from his horse and swung the door wide open. The trapper was on top of Tawanda with the flat edge of a large knife pressed against her mouth. She struggled, but the man kept her firmly pinned to the hay-covered floor.

Nicholas ran over and flung him off. The stunned trapper squinted when he saw Nicholas. He slowly rose, pitching his knife from one hand to the other.

"I thought I told you to mind your own business, mister," he sneered, swaying back and forth.

"She is my business, stranger!"

"We'll just see about that!" The man smiled wickedly and

162

lunged at Nicholas.

Nicholas pulled out his knife and with one swoop thrust it into the man's chest. The man grunted, eyes fully open. He looked at Nicholas, took one step forward, and fell dead on the floor.

Nicholas rolled the dead man over and pulled the bloody knife from his chest. He asked Tawanda if she was okay. She nodded slightly to assure him she was, although her whole body shook as she sat with her knees pressed to her chest.

"Wait here!" Nicholas said quietly. He paused before he went outside, not wanting to look suspicious. He led the horses inside and closed the barn door, allowing only a hint of light to enter.

He covered the man's body with straw and helped Tawanda on her horse. He saw blood dripping from her leg and onto the saddle blanket. He didn't know how badly she was cut, but waited to check the wound until after they rode out of the barn. Nicholas raced the horses until they reached the edge of town and thought it was safe to rest.

"Are you okay?" he asked again. More blood dripped from her leg, soaking the horse's back. Again, she nodded with assurance.

Nicholas took the reins of both horses and headed north. Fearing for their safety, he had to get to Andrew's cabin as quickly as possible.

Chapter XXV

Nicholas and Tawanda were close to Andrew's place. Fresh snow had fallen and there was a cold bite in the air. Nicholas should have smelled smoke coming from Andrew's cabin by now. Perhaps Andrew had struck out on his own to find him or to hunt down those responsible for his father's death.

As the cabin came into view through the trees, Nicholas saw that there was indeed no smoke rising from the chimney. Andrew must have been gone for some time, since he never let the fire go out in winter. But he knew that Andrew wouldn't mind if he used his place for the night, instead of traveling the extra two miles to get to his cabin. He was concerned about Tawanda and wanted to get a fire going as soon as possible.

When they reached the barn, he saw no tracks in the snow. Nicholas dismounted and opened the barn door. He walked the horses inside and couldn't believe what he saw. In the very last stall Major was standing quietly, his eyes half-closed. Nicholas rubbed the long bridge of his nose.

"Never thought I'd see you again, ol' fella," he said, smiling and checking him over.

Major looked well taken care of and he had Andrew to thank for that. After the battle at Fort Johnstown, his frightened horse must have galloped all the way back to the barn. Andrew must have been devastated to discover the rider-less horse. He probably assumed that Nicholas was killed, wounded, or being held captive. He would somehow have to find his friend to show him that he was alive and well.

Nicholas looked inside Major's stall and found something unsettling. The horse didn't have any food. Andrew would never leave home without first making sure that a penned animal had enough water to drink and plenty to eat. Something was seriously amiss.

Nicholas helped Tawanda from her horse and was relieved to see that she wasn't bleeding anymore.

"I'll get food and water for the horses, then get a fire going."

Tawanda didn't respond and sat on a hay bale while Nicholas went to work. He hated himself for not protecting her and wished he had talked her out of traveling with him. But she would have been in more danger if she went off without him.

Nicholas finished his chores. When he went to take Tawanda's hand to help her stand, she turned her shoulder and got up by herself.

"Tawanda," he said gently, "it's my fault that..." When he tried to place his hand on her shoulder, she flinched and pulled away.

"Okay," he said, letting her be.

She followed him from the barn. He was glad Major would have other horses to keep him company. And now, he needed to focus all of his attention on Tawanda.

Nicholas slowly walked toward the cabin, and Tawanda kept some distance between them. He respected her privacy and left her alone for the time being. He did it out of consideration since, what she had endured earlier, must have been a horrific experience.

It was getting dark. He lit a lantern hanging next to the cabin's door. When he opened it, a putrid smell enveloped him. Nicholas gagged.

"Wait here," he said. "An animal must have gotten in and rotted to death."

Nicholas held the lantern before him and warily stepped inside. The smell was so unbearable that he pulled up his shirt to cover his mouth and nose.

He noticed that something was terribly wrong. Most of the furniture was overturned and items were scattered about the floor.

In a corner was a blanket covering a large lump the size of a small bear. That would explain the mess, and certainly an animal that size could have entered through the front door and barricaded itself in. As Nicholas approached, the stench made him gag.

Nicholas sat a chair upright and placed his lantern atop it. Keeping his shirt over his nose, he slowly pulled away the blanket. At first he couldn't tell what it was, but then his eyes widened with horror.

Andrew's neck was severely slashed, almost completely decapitating him. Hundreds of hibernating flies had nested in the caked blood of the wound.

Nicholas ran from the cabin, cupping his mouth and holding his stomach. He leaned against the cabin with one hand and started to dry heave. He took several deep breaths before he regained his composure. Tawanda sat near the doorway, arms wrapped around her knees, rocking back and forth and humming quietly. He could see she was shivering. Nicholas went into the cabin to get her a blanket, racing back out as quickly as he could.

"Listen to me," he said, covering her, "my friend is dead. I have to bring him outside. Then I'll get you inside and make a fire."

Tawanda didn't acknowledge him and kept humming and rocking. Nicholas went back inside and started to dry heave again upon seeing the corpse. He threw another blanket on the floor, dragged Andrew's body onto it, and pulled him outside. Nicholas took him to the back of the barn, wrapped him as best he could, and covered him with some old lumber stacked next to the building. He would tend to his body in the morning, since the cold weather would preserve him until then.

He shattered the cabin's front windows with a chair to let in fresh air. He quickly had a large fire going and went back outside to get Tawanda.

She wasn't humming anymore, but still rocked back and forth, twisting one of her braids, staring blankly into the darkness. Nicholas knelt down next to her and helped her stand. This time she didn't refuse his help.

After the smell had mostly dissipated, he gathered some hides to cover the shattered windows. He rearranged the furniture that was turned over, helped Tawanda sit next to the fire, and lay himself down on a cot. He watched Tawanda stare into the fire and felt sorry for her. What had happened earlier affected her horribly. But his only real concern at the moment was to get her back to his cabin and make her as comfortable as possible. Then he drifted into a dark sleep, forgetting all about their hunger.

**

"*Nicholas*," said the familiar voice, looming from the darkness.

"*Nicholas, where are you?*"

His mother's voice was soothing to his ears, but he couldn't see her or anything around him.

"I'm here, Mother!" he said in a child-like tone. "I'm here...but I can't see you!"

"*Look harder, my prince,*" she said.

Nicholas squinted in the blackness and thought he could see someone...or something.

"Is that you, Mother?" he asked, leaning forward to get a better look.

"*Yes, my son. I've been looking for you, Nicholas. We've been looking for you!*"

Nicholas saw white forms coming toward him.

"Oh Mother, I've missed you so," he said, his arms open as he moved toward the shapes.

"*I can't give you a hug, Nicholas!*" she laughed.

Nicholas stopped and slowly lowered his arms.

"*You pulled a fast one on me, didn't you!*" she screamed. "*I'm afraid that we're going to have to punish you, my dear, dear prince!*"

Everything around him became clear, and Nicholas became terribly frightened. His mother stood before him in the same white gown he had seen so many times before. Her hair was matted with blood, the hatchet lodged deep in her skull. As she drew closer, he could see his father and Andrew directly behind her, hacked with deep cuts and gashes, their clothes soaked with blood. Major Johnson and Abraham floated in midair, legless, with weird looks of approval on their rotting faces. Swarms of flies flew from their open mouths.

"NO!" Nicholas screamed as they reached out to grab him. "I tried, Mother...I tried! Please don't!"

Nicholas sat up. His heart pounded and he was drenched in sweat. He tried to catch his breath while his mind slowly returned to a conscious state. To his relief, he saw the interior of Andrew's cabin illuminated by the fire. Before him was a portrait of Andrew in full military dress, hanging precariously on the wall. He hadn't noticed it before.

Tawanda was still sitting where he had left her. She rocked back and forth, stroking her braid that leaked blood onto the floor. She turned slowly toward him and smiled. It wasn't her face, but the trapper who had abducted her.

The thing stood up, pulled a knife from its waist, and flew toward Nicholas.

"Told ya to mind your own business, didn't I?" it squealed. The thing floated over him, its eyes as black as onyx, grinning with sharp teeth. It raised the knife high in the air and swooped down.

***

Nicholas screamed and again sat up. This time he was wide awake and looked toward the fireplace. Tawanda was gone. He got to his feet, but she was nowhere. He ran outside and yelled for her, but the only sound was the breeze whisking through the tops of the tall pines.

Standing in the center of the yard, he thought he heard a woman's voice coming from the back of the barn. He ran to the place and found Tawanda kneeling next to Andrew's makeshift grave, rocking and humming. He lifted her from the ground.

"Stay away from here!" he screamed at her. He carried her back to the cabin and gently forced her to lie down on a bed next to the fireplace. He covered her from neck to toe with a blanket and went back to his own cot. Nicholas didn't know what to do with her. There was something terribly wrong with her mental state. He felt helpless...and horribly responsible.

Nicholas sat up the remainder of the night and stared at Tawanda. Eventually she fell asleep. And as tired as he was, he couldn't do the same for fear that she would leave and he wouldn't be able to find her. He wanted all of it to be over. Life had become a miserable existence. His only salvation had been Tawanda, but that no longer brought him much comfort.

Chapter XXVI

The overcast morning finally came and Nicholas saw that Tawanda was still asleep. He went out to the barn to prepare the horses for the short trip to his cabin and to check his guns. He kept the pistol in the pack on Tawanda's horse. He would ride Major and use the other horse to carry sacks of grain and hay. Nicholas led the team out of the barn and tied them next to the cabin. He grabbed some jerky from a leather bag and a flask of water before going back inside to get her.

Tawanda was sitting up and turned to look at him. At least she was aware of his presence. He sat next to her and offered her some of the jerky. She silently took it from him and they both ate.

"As soon as we finish eating, we'll be heading north," he said, offering her the flask of water. "About two miles from here is my home...*our* home," he corrected himself and put an arm around her. "I'm going to take care of you." He kissed her lightly on the forehead. Tawanda didn't appear to notice the affectionate gesture and continued to eat.

After breakfast, Nicholas hoisted Tawanda on her horse and led the caravan on foot to the beginning of the trail that cut through the forest. Then he returned to the back of the barn and dragged Andrew's body back to the cabin. He drenched the corpse and the interior with whatever lantern fuel was left, lit some papers, and set everything on fire.

The flames rose quickly and grew hot. Nicholas went to the door and looked at his friend one last time before shutting it tightly behind him. He couldn't help but feel responsible because of his selfishness. If only he had waited.

Nicholas walked back to Tawanda and turned to watch the cabin burn. Flames and smoke engulfed the interior and seeped through the shattered windows. He looked to the heavens and asked for his God to accept and watch over him. He hopped up on Major and put his horse next to hers.

169

"Tawanda, I know you can hear me. Do you remember what I said about the pistol? Please let me know that you understand what I told you to do."

Tawanda looked at him and barely nodded. Satisfied with the slight response, he entered the trail. Nicholas thought there might be nothing left to go to, but there was no way of telling until they got there.

The east lake of Garoga was barely visible as they got closer to Nicholas's property. He decided to cut through the woods and let the horses drink at the water's edge so he wouldn't have to worry about them later. Even if his cabin were as he had left it, there would still be much to do before the evening approached. He didn't think that Tawanda would be much help...and didn't want her to be. He wanted to make her as comfortable as possible, so she could hopefully put everything in the past and they could have a peaceful life together.

Nicholas guided the horses steadily through the trees and then stopped unexpectedly. He saw an Indian squatting next to the water's edge—his horse nearby. Major grew nervous and pranced about, letting out a short whimper. Upon hearing the horse, the Indian stood up and turned around. Nicholas looked him in the eyes and saw a blue, wing-shaped mark on his forehead. The Indian leapt onto his horse and headed back into the woods.

"Stay here!" Nicholas yelled to Tawanda and jabbed his heels into Major's sides.

Nicholas kept sight of him as they galloped through the trees. Major was riled with fury and Nicholas had to duck several low branches that almost knocked him to the ground. Nicholas kept close behind until they reached the clearing where his cabin stood.

He let go of the reins and reached for his musket. He cocked the hammer, put the stock of the gun to his chin, and squeezed the trigger. The Indian fell to the ground at the clearing's edge.

At the sound of gunshot, three warriors with the same mark ran out of the cabin. Nicholas saw them, threw down his musket, and rode toward them at full gallop. Nicholas sat forward on Major's neck and pulled back on the reins with all his might. Major reared, and on the way down the horse's hooves knocked the first Indian to the ground. Nicholas jumped off his horse and was on top of him in an instant. He felt a sharp jab penetrate his leg as he bashed in the Indian's skull with a large stone. The second attacker, wielding a hatchet, yelped and rushed him. Nicholas stepped to the side, grabbed his arm with both hands, and twisted the hatchet into his gut. Just then he heard a shot ring out and turned to see the last Indian only inches from his back.

The Indian landed hard on top of Nicholas and they toppled to the ground. Nicholas looked into his face, saw he was dead, and threw the Indian off him. Tawanda stood a few feet away, holding the smoking pistol in both hands. She dropped to the muddy snow, staring at Nicholas.

Nicholas tried to get up but couldn't bend his leg. The first attacker had stabbed him. He crawled over to Tawanda and held her tightly, his chin resting atop her head.

"It's over now," he said, kissing the top of her head.

Yet it didn't really seem over. All of those years of mental anguish and waiting...waiting for justice and some peace in his life to finally come. How he longed for revenge so that he could mourn and put it all behind him. It seemed too artificial, to wait so long only to have all of it end within minutes.

Tawanda helped him as he struggled to get up. She held him as tightly as she could as he limped to the cabin. It wasn't a serious wound, but it was enough to cause him a great deal of discomfort.

Inside, the cabin was pretty much as he left it. Somewhat in disarray, yet nothing was really out of place. Tawanda sat him on his bed and found some water and a cloth to clean and bandage him. Nicholas saw a jug of whiskey on the table and asked her to get it for him. He drank two large gulps, and not long after forgot about the pain. He drank until he felt he could go back outside to finish the grisly business of dragging the dead Indians into the barn. Tawanda helped him with the gruesome chore before rounding up the horses. Nicholas would take their corpses to town the next day. He had to hand them over to the proper authorities, since he was sure they were wanted in many parts of the area.

That evening, Tawanda seemed to be more herself and made them a meal from meat and corn that had been stored by the savages. Nicholas came to the assumption that they were responsible for Andrew's death. He figured that the renegades made quarters in his

171

cabin on the reckoning that it was abandoned, and decided to use it as a hunting lodge on their way to and from Canada. He felt remorseful that if he had never left, Andrew still might be alive. He had been only days from saving him.

That night, and for the first time in quite a while, Nicholas slept peacefully. There were no dreams or nightmares that he could remember. Maybe, he thought, there was some closure after all.

In the morning, Nicholas felt much better as he limped to the barn. He saddled Major and threw some provisions over his back for the trip. One by one, he picked up each Indian and threw them onto the backs of their horses. He didn't want to leave Tawanda, but had no choice... and he wasn't about to risk another incident like the last time they were in town.

Before leaving, he held Tawanda as tightly as he could while she limply held him back.

"I won't leave unless I know that you will be all right by yourself," he said, looking into her eyes. And for the first time since they left the Mohawk village, she spoke to him.

"I will be fine. You must go and not worry," she said and hugged him a little harder. "I will wait for your return."

Nicholas let her go and stepped toward the door. "Don't go anywhere, and secure the door when I leave," he firmly ordered. "The musket and pistol are ready if you need them. I'll be back before the sun rises."

Nicholas didn't want to waste any more daylight and stepped out into morning sun. The door latched behind him and he went to the barn.

He tied the reins of the three horses together and led the team south. He passed by what was Andrew's place and saw that the smoldering cabin had completely burned to the ground. He kept the barn standing in case he would need it in the future. Funny, but he didn't think that Andrew would mind.

He made it to Fort Johnstown within half the day and went right to the local jail. He showed the Indians to the Marshall and was offered quite a reward for their capture and their horses. Nicholas kept one of the horses and immediately put the money to good use. He went to the trading post at the far end of town and made many purchases.

He bought provisions for himself and Tawanda, and purchased a small wagon with two mules. It wasn't much to look at, but he thought it would do the job.

The wagon was loaded with blankets, food, gunpowder, and skins. He spent almost all of the reward money, and before leaving he made it a point to speak with the proprietor.

"I need someone that will deliver these goods for me," he said, checking over his bill of sale. "Someone I can rely on and a man that knows the land. Anyone come to mind?"

"Well," the merchant said, playing with his whiskers, "there's ol' Sergeant Tom who might be able to help you out. He used to trap these parts before the war. Ever since he was discharged, he doesn't do much except beg for money so he can get a drink or two at the tavern. Good man...and most people like him...just feel sorry for him."

"Is that where I'll find him? The tavern?" Nicholas asked.

"Suppose you will. I'm sure of it."

Nicholas thanked him and tied Major and the other horse to the wagon and drove the team up the street. He pulled in front of the tavern, locked the wagon's brake, and went inside. He noticed a short gray-haired fellow with raggedy clothes begging the barkeep for a small sample of liquor.

"Just one, Silas!" he begged. "As soon as I get a pelt to trade, you know I'll be good for it!"

"Tom, you know I can't give you any more. As it is, you haven't paid for the last three," the proprietor told him as he wiped a glass clean. "As soon as you get some money I'll reconsider, but for now..."

"Pardon me, Gents," interjected Nicholas, and both looked at him as if he were disrupting a formal engagement. Nicholas threw a coin on the bar.

"I'd like a drink of your best whiskey and one for my friend...whatever he desires."

The barkeep grabbed a bottle from the shelf, never once taking his eye off Nicholas.

"Same for me," the old man said, also keeping one eye on him.

The old timer raised his glass high to toast Nicholas before greedily swigging the whiskey down.

"One more, friend?" he asked Nicholas, wiping alcohol from his white beard.

"Why not?" said Nicholas, and they gulped down another shot.

"Name's Tom...Sergeant Tom is what they call me. Who do I owe this favor to?" he said with a toothless grin, and added, "And don't you worry, sir, I'm good for it!"

"Name's not important at the moment," said Nicholas, "though I do have some urgent business that needs tending to...if you're interested."

The old man looked him up and down. "Nah," he muttered, waving his hand and turned to face the front of the bar. "Not interested."

Nicholas threw some money on the bar. "Five pieces of silver now, and ten after the job is done."

The man gave Nicholas a strange look. "Who do you want killed, mister, 'cause I ain't the type to..."

"Nothing like that at all!" chuckled Nicholas. "I need a very important delivery made and you come highly recommended, my good fellow!"

Not one to be out-haggled, the man squinted one eye and said, "Throw in a bottle and I guess we have a deal."

Nicholas laughed and motioned for the bartender to give him a bottle of whiskey. The old man cackled while reaching for it. Nicholas grabbed it and pulled it away.

"You'll get the bottle after the job is done!" Nicholas said. "Only then will you get the rest of the money and the whiskey, my good man. You have my word of honor that they'll be waiting for you."

The man was skeptical, but didn't hesitate to stick out his hand.

"Deal, Mister! If I might," he asked suspiciously, "what's so important that would make a man pay so handsomely?"

"Come with me," said Nicholas, and they exited the building.

Nicholas showed him the wagon and gave him explicit instructions.

"There's a Mohawk village southwest of here at the river. Do you know of it?"

"Surely do! I trapped those parts for quite a spell before I entered the war."

"Good," said Nicholas. "Can you speak their language?"

"I'm a little rusty, but know it good enough to get by."

"That'll do fine, and make your job easier," Nicholas said. "See to it that these goods get to that village. The contents of the wagon are for Chief Manendra and the horse is for his son, Alok. If any of the warriors greet you, tell them your business with all honesty and that you have been sent by White Bear. They'll know the name. Can you remember all of this?"

The man stood up straight and proclaimed, "My body may be old and brittle, but my head is sharper than a woodsman's axe!"

Nicholas smiled at him. "Then it would be appreciated if you could start out this very moment."

The man cackled and said, "Fairly well, young sir," and climbed onto the wagon. Nicholas untied Major and mounted him.

"One more thing," said Nicholas, "Do you know where the east and west lakes of Garoga meet?"

"Never been there, but know its proximity."

"After you make the delivery, bring the wagon and team to my home. Just follow the north trail. I'm two miles northwest of a burned-out cabin. You can't miss it."

The old man tipped his hat, released the brake, and snapped the reins. And Nicholas wasted no more time setting out for his cabin and getting back to Tawanda.

Chapter XXVII

Nicholas pushed Major as fast as the beast could run, only stopping twice along the way to rest. He didn't want to leave Tawanda in her fragile state and it seemed like the trip back took forever. He rode hard into the late night hours and, as promised, made it back before the sun rose.

He didn't even bother to take Major to the barn. Instead, he jumped off the horse and ran to the door. It was locked from the inside and Nicholas beat his fists against it.

"Tawanda!" he yelled. "It's me...Nicholas!"

He heard the board that secured the door being lifted. The door creaked open a tiny bit and then Tawanda let him in. He gave her a big hug and kissed her cheek. He was so relieved to see that she was all right. He hesitantly let go of her and sat at the table to take off his boots. Seeing how tired he was, Tawanda went over to the fireplace where she had some food prepared. She brought it over and set it in front of him. Nicholas placed his hand on hers and smiled. She let him hold it there for a short moment before pulling away to go back to the fireplace.

Tawanda sat at the other end of the table while Nicholas ate and talked.

"I sent Manendra some supplies...and a horse for Alok," he said in between bites. "I bought some provisions to last us a while, and oh..." He went outside in his stocking feet to grab his pack from Major. He returned with a package and placed it next to her. She stared at it while her hands fidgeted under the table.

"Go ahead!" he said, pushing the package closer to her. "It's for you! Open it!"

Tawanda untied the twine that bound the package and opened it. She lifted a colorful silk wrap from the paper and rubbed the soft fabric against her cheek. Then she unfolded it and wrapped it around her shoulders. She smiled slightly and rose to give him a hug. Nicholas could see that she was pleased. Then she crossed the room to lie down and he went to her.

"We will have a happy life together, if you put your faith in me," he said as he sat on her bed and rubbed her arm.

He could see that she was exhausted and told her to rest, while he took care of things. He led Major to the barn and returned to the cabin. Nicholas was glad to be home with her, and after a short while, he too fell asleep just as the sun started to rise. He dreamed about their new life together and how things would be in the future. It was a happy dream, unlike the ones that had plagued him in the past.

Things were pretty ordinary for the next week, until Nicholas heard horses on the trail, along with high-pitched whistling. He came out from the barn and saw Sergeant Tom driving a team and empty wagon into the yard.

"Well, I'll be," said Nicholas, grabbing hold of the tired mules. "Didn't think you'd make it, Tom," he said with a broad smile.

"Good for my word," Tom said, getting down and shaking Nicholas's hand. "Had a courtship with a couple ladies," he said, as he grinned and winked. "Problem is, they got stuck in a bottle, an' ol' Tom is too much a gentleman to see 'em held prisoner…so I let 'em out!" he said with a cackle.

"Well," Nicholas said, "help me get this team in the barn and I'll introduce you to my wife and a lady that might need help getting out of a jug."

"Now that, sir, is an invite I'll never turn down!" Tom winked again at Nicholas and cackled even harder.

After the mules were placed in separate stalls and fed, Nicholas took him inside to meet Tawanda. The old sergeant took off his hat at the sight of her and exclaimed in English, "So this is the Indian princess I heard about!" He held out his hand to take hers. Tawanda looked at Nicholas for approval before offering her hand.

"My name is Thomas, ma'am," he said in broken Mohawk. "I am honored to be in your home."

Nicholas smiled and politely said, "Please have a seat, Tom."

They sat down, and over drinks Tom told him how some Mohawk warriors intercepted him when he neared the village.

"Just like you said, I mentioned the name White Bear and they escorted me right into the center of that camp. I told the chief,

Manendra, that these were the gifts of White Bear, and he led me to one of their houses where we talked for some time. That's how I found out that you had once lived there and that you married his daughter."

"Did the chief's son accept the horse as a gift?" Nicholas asked.

"Funny you should mention that, because at first it seemed to me that he was angry with the idea and just up an' left me and the chief sittin' there with our mouths open. Then he came back and said to give this to you."

Tom reached in his pocket, pulled out a stone, and handed it to Nicholas.

"It doesn't seem to be much at first look. Maybe you can tell me what it means."

Nicholas held the round, smooth quartz in his hand and looked at it with much affection. It wasn't much, but in Nicholas's mind it meant a great deal.

"It's a fishing stone," he said, barely hearing his own words. "Alok, the chief's son and I, used to hunt, trap, and fish together as boys. This was his favorite stone and no one was allowed to use it. He had it all these years," said Nicholas more so to himself, as he rolled it between his fingers.

Nicholas knew then that all ill feelings between the two of them were undoubtedly forgotten.

He got up and placed the stone on the hearth of the fireplace. "I can't thank you enough for taking care of my business, Tom," he said, pouring him another drink, "which is why I have a proposition to make you."

Tom took another drink and waited for him to explain.

"I have a claim of many acres in these parts to hunt and trap, or to do as I wish, but I can't do it alone. I need someone to stay on with me...not just to help me with my traps, but for security purposes."

"Security purposes?" echoed Tom.

"For Tawanda," he said. "There are times when I'll be in the woods or taking the occasional trip to town, and I'll need someone to watch over her while I'm away. Whoever I hire will receive, at no expense, lodging and meals in exchange for said security...and for help with the trapping. Profit made from the pelts will be divvied at an eighty to twenty split...eighty for me and twenty for the hired hand."

Tom stroked his beard while Nicholas talked.

"What do you say, Tom?" he asked, leaning forward. "An experienced trapper such as yourself could become somewhat wealthy over a short period of time."

Tom leaned back and thought for a moment. "Would be nice to get back in the mountains again." He made a squint with his eye and said, "Sixty to your forty?"

"Seventy-five to your twenty-five, and one bottle a week on, let's say, the Sabbath?"

Tom, never one to be out-haggled, leaned in further and said, "Seventy to my thirty," now squinting both eyes, "*and* the bottle to celebrate the Almighty."

Nicholas sat back, pretended to think hard about the offer, and then stuck out his hand. "Done!" he said.

Tom cackled harder than before and returned the handshake. "You could learn a bit when negotiatin'...but not bad, though."

In no time at all, the sergeant fit right in and settled into a comfortable loft in the barn. Within a few weeks, Nicholas knew that he had made the right decision. Tom was a very good trapper and taught Nicholas many new ways to easily capture all sorts of game. And as promised, Nicholas shared the profits made on the pelts every month and made sure that Tom received his bottle every Sunday, which Tom used to full advantage.

One Sunday in late spring, Tom was full of liquor as he staggered toward the field where Nicholas was preparing the soil for a new crop. He stopped and thought he saw an Indian on horseback at the wood's edge. He ran as fast as his unsteady legs could carry him and yelled to warn Nicholas of the intruder. Nicholas looked to where he was pointing and there, in fact, was an Indian watching them. Nicholas recognized the horse that he had given to Alok as a gift. He threw his hand up in the air to show Alok that he knew he was there and watching him.

This went on every so often throughout the year, and instead of raising an arm to acknowledge his adopted brother, Alok would turn around and go back into the forest. Nicholas assumed that Alok was keeping an eye on his sister. And although Alok disagreed with his sister's choices, he still loved her and cared about her welfare.

Nicholas worried about Tawanda more and more as the weeks turned into months. She cooked for the both of them and took charge of many of the chores around the home, but was still distant toward Nicholas, especially during the evening hours when he yearned to get close to her in an intimate way. Every night ended the same. He would lie in his bed while she was in hers. He never tried to force himself on her, yet he longed for the day when they could plan to have children.

Months went by and he noticed that her body and face were swelling to a rapid degree. Her circulation must have been poor, since August and September were extremely warm and she insisted on wearing her full leather outfit. Either she didn't want to expose the upper part of her body—as the women of the Mohawk did in the hot summer months—with Tom in such close vicinity, or perhaps it was because she was still scarred by the assault months ago. Whatever the cause, something was very wrong with her, but when Nicholas asked if she was feeling alright, Tawanda would tell him she was fine or avoid the subject altogether.

It wasn't until late October that he grew gravely concerned. She was frequently getting sick to her stomach and would run a high fever on and off. At one point, the sickness and fever kept her in bed for a day or two.

One evening in November, when Nicholas returned from his traps, he found Tom sitting next to her as she lay in bed, writhing and moaning in pain. Nicholas raced to her side.

"Tawanda?" Nicholas said, holding her cool, clammy hand.

"She can't hear you," said Tom, pressing a damp cloth to her forehead. "Maybe she can, but I've been trying to get her to say somethin' ever since I brought her inside."

Nicholas looked at Tom and didn't understand. "Brought her inside?" he repeated. "What happened while I was gone?"

"I was in the barn tending to the animals, and when I went outside, I found her lying in the yard. Fainted right there, I reckon'. I picked her up and she's been here for about two hours or so."

Nicholas looked at her as she squirmed in her bed. "What do you think is wrong, Tom?"

Tom wiped his forehead with the back of his forearm. "Seen

this once before," he said in a low voice, while dipping the rag in some water and wringing it out. "Years ago, a whole Indian village got "the fever" and most of 'em died. The ones that lived blamed it on the settlers, saying that it was them that carried the sickness. This looks like what I saw when I trapped nearby and went into their camp to trade with them. I tried to help, but there wasn't much to do except wait it out and hope for the best."

Tom got up to stretch his back. "She's a strong woman, Nick," he said with a positive tone, placing a hand on his shoulder. "Just have to make her as comfortable as possible."

Nicholas looked up at Tom. "How long? I mean, how long was it before they succumbed to the sickness?"

Tom didn't want to tell him how bad the illness really was, but thought he owed it to him to be honest. "It could be three...maybe four days."

Nicholas's heart sank. He couldn't just wait to see if she would live or die. He had to do something, or come up with some kind of solution.

"Tomorrow is Sunday, and if I leave for town now I can get there in the early morning before most are attending services. With any luck I'll be able to find the doctor."

Nicholas looked at Tom for approval, but his hired hand only stood there scratching his head while looking down at Tawanda.

"Couldn't hurt none," Tom finally said. "You'd better git goin'!" he urged. "I'll keep an eye on her."

After kissing her on the forehead, Nicholas grabbed what he needed and went to get Major.

"Run as fast as you can, ol' boy," he said to his horse, as they rode off into the night.

Tom knew it was bad. He didn't want to tell Nicholas that if her fever went higher or didn't break, he didn't think she would survive the night. It was better that he didn't say anything. That way, Nicholas wouldn't blame himself for not doing anything if something was to happen to her.

Tom grabbed a bottle of whiskey from the cupboard. Under the circumstances, he didn't think that Nicholas would mind if he was paid a little earlier than usual. He opened the bottle and took a large swig while sitting next to her. He tried to keep her cool as he sponged her arms and face with fresh water. It would be a long night.

"God's speed," he said quietly. "God's speed."

Chapter XXVIII

Nicholas reached the town and went straight to the doctor's house. He pounded hard on the door. After a short wait, he could see the interior of the house flicker with light.

"Who's out there?" called a man's voice from behind the door.

"It's Nicholas Dunne...and I need a doctor!"

The man grumbled a few inaudible words before the door unlatched and opened slightly. Nicholas saw a young fellow holding out a candle.

"It's a little early for a livestock call," he said with a yawn. "Whatever it is, I'm sure that it can wait a few more hours, can't it?"

"It's my wife!" Nicholas replied with urgency. "She's fallen sick with a fever and I need your help!"

The young doctor stood motionless for a moment and then invited him in. "What are her symptoms?" he asked.

"Stomach sickness...fever...fainting spells. Please, we have to hurry! I live some miles from here and I'm afraid she may not have much time!"

The doctor sighed heavily. He told Nicholas to go to the carriage house, prepare his horse and buggy, and bring it out front. In the meantime he would get dressed and get his surgical bag.

Outside, the doctor climbed into the buggy and followed Nicholas out of town. Major trotted alongside the carriage while the doctor needled Nicholas for more information on Tawanda's condition. Nicholas told him Tom's story about the fever that swept through an Indian village.

"I do remember the story as a child," the doctor said. "It was the "puerperal epidemic" if I remember correctly, but the Indians have adapted quite well to the sickness over the years. Could be Scarlet Fever, I suppose, but there haven't been any unusual outbreaks lately. I do have another hunch as to what it might be, although I won't be able to come to any conclusions until I examine her."

Nicholas couldn't understand what he was implying and didn't really care at the moment. He could only think of getting back to her as quickly as possible. Meanwhile, the doctor kept talking and realized that Nicholas was only half listening, as he had to repeat his questions two or three times.

It was almost light out when they passed by the remains of Andrew's cabin. The doctor was pretty sure at this point where they were headed and remembered something that he had longed to forget, although the incident prompted him to enter the field of medicine.

When he was a young man—barely in his teens—his father and uncles had talked of a gruesome massacre that took place near where they presently were. He was pretty sure that Dunne was the surname of the unfortunate ones. Whenever it was mentioned in their home, his mother would quickly shuffle him off to his room so he couldn't overhear the men talking. Without her knowing, he would creep from his room to the top of the stairs and listen as they told of how the poor, unsuspecting settlers were hacked to death by savage Indians. He also remembered that a boy was missing, who turned up not long after with a Mohawk tribe that lived to the southwest and along the river. He would lie in bed at night, not understanding how people could be sacrificed in such a manner, and vowed to himself that he would someday do whatever he could to help those in need.

The doctor always wondered what became of the little boy, who had lost so much at such a tender age. By putting two and two together, he had his answer. And he was glad to be able to do something for him, and if his hunch was correct, things could turn out to be very positive.

The sun had barely risen over the mountain tops when they arrived at the cabin. Nicholas jumped off Major's back and told the doctor that he would meet him inside. The doctor didn't even make it to the front door before Nicholas rushed outside and hurried to the barn. The doctor was startled and went into the cabin to check on his patient. He discovered why Nicholas was so alarmed. There was no one inside.

The bed in which she had apparently been lying was soaked with water and blood. A sense of dread filled him.

Nicholas swung open the barn door and found Tom snoring on some hay with an empty bottle lying next to him. Nicholas kicked his feet.

"Tom!" he screamed and kicked him harder, but Tom only stirred a little and went back to snoring. Nicholas looked around the barn, fetched a bucket of water, and threw it in his face. Tom jerked with a start.

"Wha's that?" he responded.

Nicholas reached down, grabbed the front of his shirt, and shook him.

"Tom!" he yelled, slapping his cheeks. "Wake up!"

Tom barely opened his eyes. "Nick?" he muttered. "Wha's wrong?"

"Tawanda!" he screamed at him. "Where's Tawanda!"

Tom didn't understand him at first. "Who?" he mumbled, then started to drift back to sleep.

Nicholas shook his upper body hard enough to rattle his brain. "Tawanda!" he yelled again. "Where's Tawanda? You must remember!"

Tom could hardly raise his arm and point. "She's in the cabin, Nick," he stammered. "Her fever broke, and I mus've fallen asleep."

Nicholas pushed him back down. He ran outside and called out for her, racing around each building in desperation. The doctor watched him. That's when he saw the tiniest droplet of blood in the snow. He investigated further and found another small droplet, and then many more that seemed to lead toward the woods.

The doctor pointed toward the trees. "She's in the woods somewhere!" he yelled out.

Nicholas swung around and sprinted past the doctor to the direction he was pointing.

"Tawanda!" he yelled out as he entered the forest. "Tawanda!"

Nicholas came to a halt when he saw her in the near distance, sitting with her back against a tree. He ran over to her, with the doctor close on his heels, and dropped to his knees next to her rigid body. He was unaware of anything around him except for what was in front of him.

He looked into her frozen, half-open eyes. Her skin, once tan and void of any imperfection, was now colorless. Her head was almost completely bald. Clumps of black hair lay on top of the frosty ground.

Her rigid arms were closed around a small bundle that rested upon her lap.

Nicholas trembled as he peeled away the frozen wrap to uncover what was hidden underneath. He didn't notice that the doctor knelt next to him, and barely heard him speak.

"It was a boy," the doctor said in a low, gentle voice as he inspected the small body. "Stillborn, most likely," he added, knowing all too well that that wasn't the case. He had seen infants asphyxiated before and could make the diagnosis from the abnormally blue color of the baby's lips. The doctor ruled out the umbilical cord as the culprit, due to the fact that it was still attached and nowhere near the baby's neck. The only other way that an infant could suffocate was only if the mother rolled onto the baby as they slept, which was not the case at all.

Nicholas didn't tell the doctor that the baby wasn't his. It didn't matter. He failed to protect her, as he had promised. Everything that mattered to him was gone. Nicholas held Tawanda tightly in his arms and rocked her back and forth.

"It's over now," he said, laying his head on hers. "You can rest peacefully now," he said to her, and it was the last time he ever felt the need to cry.

The doctor left him alone with her and headed back toward the cabin where he met up with Tom. Tom knew right away what had happened, and as the doctor placed a hand on his shoulder, Tom drew away and went to the barn for a pick and shovel. He felt incredibly responsible for her death, and the least he could do was to dig the grave. It would be one of the last jobs he carried out for Nicholas before he left.

After some time, the doctor left the cabin and met up with Nicholas, who was carrying the lifeless bodies from the woods toward the opposite side of the field. Tom sat on a log waiting for them, shivering in the cold. He had dug a shallow grave in the frozen earth next to a single tree that stood out from the rest. Nicholas placed the bodies in the grave and covered them with the blanket that once concealed the infant. The doctor said a short sermon before the first spade of dirt was shoveled over them. Nicholas knelt next to the mound and laid his chest and arms over it. Tom and the doctor eventually helped him to his feet and led him back into the cabin.

After helping Nicholas to his bed and seeing that there wasn't much else he could do, the doctor climbed back into his wagon. Before he left, Tom stepped out of the doorway.

"He's going to need you the most now," the doctor said with great sorrow. "Tell him that there's no payment due, and if there's anything...anything at all..."

Tom nodded to him with his head down. With that, the doctor snapped the reins and drove the carriage toward the trail.

Tom didn't know how he could live with himself after what happened, and vowed to God that he would never let another drink pass his lips. He promised to help his friend however he could, but knew that the time would eventually come for him to leave.

He entered the cabin to watch over Nicholas, failing to notice Alok in the distance. A tear ran down the Indian's cheek as he turned his horse and disappeared into the dark forest.

In time, Nicholas did manage to conquer his grief enough in order to go on, but his life was nothing more than an empty shell. He kept himself busy while Tom trapped for him and helped him with as many chores as his old and tired body could handle. That is, until it was time for him to leave. Nicholas didn't want him to go, but he also wanted to live the rest of his life in solitude...so no one else would suffer at his expense.

Nicholas gave Tawanda's horse to Tom, and met him at the barn as he was just about to depart for good.

"It's not your fault...you know that, don't you Tom?" Nicholas said, with as much kindness as he could muster.

Tom stopped tightening the horse's saddle for a moment and looked down, barely able to speak. "None of this would have come to pass if I wasn't so careless. You're a good man, Nick," he said sincerely. "Only the good Lord knows how sorry I am...and I hope you can forgive me."

Nicholas patted him a couple times on the shoulder. Tom got on the horse and left without another word. And that was the last Nicholas ever saw him, and as the years rolled by, he thought of him from time to time. He heard that Tom went back to begging and living out of a bottle, which was probably for the best. Nicholas hoped that by doing so, he was able to live out the rest of his life as peacefully as possible.

Nicholas, on the other hand, found that keeping occupied kept him sober and awake most of the time. It was the nights that he dreaded, when Tawanda would join the others...to haunt his sleep.

Chapter XXIX

Every year since Tawanda's death, Alok would appear in the spring when Nicholas was preparing the earth, and Nicholas would raise his hand to acknowledge him. Alok only watched him, as if checking to see if he was all right, before turning back into the forest. Nicholas thought of Manendra's words—how his son had a good heart and in time would prove it. And Nicholas knew that now.

Manendra had long since passed, and at the time of his death Alok was elected by the women of the tribe to be their new chief. As a leader of his people, and a good one from what Nicholas could gather, Alok's heart quickly softened, and he proved it by checking in on his step-brother every year. That is, until Nicholas decided to join the war.

Nicholas was hardened with age and could barely remember how old he was when the British invaded America in 1812. He was somewhere in his fifties, that he did know. And when the American military called on him to be one of their leading scouts, he readily accepted the job. He could see great promise in the future of his country and wanted to help preserve it. Besides, it was a way to see how the young nation had developed since the first war, not to mention that it would be an easier living than tromping through the woods, or breaking hardened land with a plow. And it really didn't matter if he lived or died. Those feelings were long behind him.

On the day of his departure, he buttoned up the cabin and barn and saddled up Patriot, his horse. He was the offspring of his last horse, Banner, who was still alive and well. Nicholas sold him to his neighbor and could visit him from time to time. He would wait by the fence and Banner would trot over to him whenever Nicholas whistled. Nicholas always had a carrot or two to give him, accompanied by an affectionate pat on his neck. He couldn't think of a better home for him to live out the remaining years of his life.

Before Banner was Major, who was long since gone and buried out back. By putting Major and his offspring out to stud, it helped keep the memory of his father alive. Like many of the people that came and

189

went in his life, he missed Major just as much as he did them.

He didn't worry too much about his property. In the past few years he had acquired more neighbors who would visit him from time to time. His closest neighbor, and the one he frequented the most, was Charles Sutter, who stopped by his home from time to time on his way to town. He would spend the night with Nicholas and over drinks would listen to the old timer's tales. Charles thought he made up most of the stories, yet enjoyed listening to him anyway. Nicholas liked him right from the start, since he was a trapper like himself. And he really did enjoy the company after years of living alone with only occasional visits to town.

Charles didn't enlist because he had a wife and children to provide for. He assured Nicholas that he'd watch the place for him while he was gone. Nicholas was grateful, and told Charles to claim the property as his own if he didn't return.

"You'll come back," he told Nicholas. "You're too old to get yourself killed."

Nicholas supposed there was a lot of truth to it. After all, if his God hadn't taken him by now, then he didn't suppose there was a reason to put him in the ground just yet. Nevertheless, Nicholas made out a second will, the first having been consumed in the fire that devoured Andrew's cabin.

Charles turned out to be right. Nicholas went through the war without incident and returned to tell his friend all about it. When Nicholas visited his neighbor, Charles's wife always made it special for him. Their children would run at him shouting, "Grandpa Nick is here!" before Nicholas even had the chance to dig through his leather pockets for the candy he always seemed to have for them.

Nicholas felt like he was part of the family, and they considered him just as much—almost to the point that no one really could remember if they were related or not, which is why Charles became upset with him on one of his visits to Nicholas's place.

One day in spring, Charles pulled his wagon into the yard and didn't find Nicholas anywhere near the cabin or barn. It wasn't long before he found him in the back of the property, digging up some earth in the nearby field.

"You're gonna kill yourself if you keep that up, ol' man,"

Charles scolded, as if Nicholas were a child getting into some sort of mischief.

"Daah," said Nicholas, waving an arm as he leaned on his shovel to take a breather.

"I'm not ready to bury you yet, so you better listen to me," hollered Charles. "I'd like some company on the way to town...if you're up to it."

"Who's buyin'?"

"Suppose I am if it will convince you to come!" Charles said with a laugh.

Nicholas looked around and then back at Charles. "Suppose there isn't any hurry to get this done. Besides, it seems like you made up my mind for me."

They started walking back toward the cabin and Nicholas paused.

"Almost forgot...since the subject of my passing on has come up, there's something I need to show you," Nicholas said with a smile.

"Sure," said Charles, a little puzzled. "What is it?"

Nicholas motioned for Charles to follow him.

They went to the far side of the field and Nicholas showed him the grave. A cracked and weathered marker read:

My Beloved Tawanda
b. 176? - d. 1783
R I P

"Didn't think to add the child to it, since it hadn't a name," Nicholas said, as he bent over and plucked a dandelion from the earth and threw it on the grave. "Didn't reckon' that it mattered much at the time."

Nicholas led Charles a few feet away to a second marker with only a single inscription:

MAJOR

"I never did bring anyone here since she died. And there's a good reason why you're here now."

Charles was surprised to see the graves. He thought all of Nick's stories might be true after all.

Nicholas walked over to the first site and knelt down to brush back the earth next to his wife's grave. There, he exposed some wooden planks that covered a pit just large and deep enough for a man to rest in.

"This is where I'll want my bones," Nicholas said, wiping his hands on his pants. "And all of this land around you will be yours."

Charles began to interrupt him, but Nicholas waved him off.

"Promise me that you will do this for me when the day comes, Charles. You and your kin are the only family I can call my own."

"And you always will be," Charles said, putting his arm around him and looking at the grave.

"The papers to my property are in a metal box under the floor. You won't have any trouble finding it."

"Okay," said Charles, feeling uncomfortable about the whole idea. Quick to change the subject, he blurted, "Now, about that trip to town. Who's buying again?"

As they walked back to the house, Charles thought he saw an Indian watching them from the edge of the woods, but when he turned his head to get a better look no one was there.

Nicholas kept his eyes in front and said to him, "That was my Indian step-brother. He's no harm. He likes to check up on me from time to time. Darned if I know why he never waves back, though," he said with a chuckle.

Charles was more intrigued than ever with the old man. "Tell me more about your step-brother on the way to town, will you?"

Nicholas laughed and told him the familiar story once again. Stories that he would tell Charles's wife and children throughout the following year, until the spring melted the snow and the earth was soft enough for a shovel to break through.

Nicholas supposed that spring was his favorite season. There was so much life that time of year, and after a long, hard winter, he was always glad to step out into the morning sun and feel its warmth on his face. And he was never disappointed to see Alok atop his horse, watching over him.

That spring, Nicholas worked the soil harder than he ever had.

Too hard, perhaps. And like many times before, he would sense someone watching him and look up. Of course it was Alok. And again, as he always did, he raised his hand. And this time, instead of turning to leave, Alok raised his. Nicholas felt an incredible peace wash over his body and saw that Alok wasn't alone.

A pure white horse came out from behind him. It was then that Nicholas saw the most beautiful Indian girl he had ever seen ride toward him in all her glory. Her smile seemed to light up the earth, as the heavens radiated down upon her.

Nicholas dropped his shovel and walked toward her. Upon reaching her, he looked up and smiled as he took Tawanda's hand in his. Together they traveled to the edge of the field, toward all that he loved…and to all who waited for him.

Alok slowly lowered his arm, as the last tear of his life left his eye. He turned his horse and melted back into the forest, never to return again.

Charles did as he promised. He found Nicholas in the field and took his worn and fragile body and placed it next to hers. He never used the land as long as he lived. The cabin and other buildings just sat and rotted with time. It was a sacred thing. That was all…nothing more.

For years, and whenever he got the chance, Charles would tell a story, to anyone who would listen, about a man once called White Bear, who bore more hardships than any man should ever have had to endure in one's lifetime. And although he suffered through it all with hardly a complaint, he did so with great sacrifice.

Today, the names of the lakes where Nicholas once lived have slightly changed. But if one follows the old Adirondack trail to the north, the one that passes near the present east lake of Caroga, one might stumble upon the remnants of a crumbled chimney, the rotted beams of a barn long decayed, the resting place of memories...and the ghosts that still haunt them, for all eternity.

End